A *Jilted Bride* FOR THE COWBOY

SWEET RIVER RANCH ROMANCE - BOOK 2

VALERIE COMER

GreenWords Media

CHAPTER ONE

The last place on the planet Graham Sullivan wanted to be on a sultry June evening was in the courtyard of his aunt and uncle's lavish home in Hinsdale with ten guys he barely knew.

Well, he did know his cousin Paul. Not that they'd ever been close, and the fact that Paul had effortlessly nabbed the girl Graham had a crush on back in college hadn't helped. Not that Paul had been aware. Cadence probably hadn't, either.

Why was Graham such a misfit? He didn't mesh much better with his cousins on his dad's side, but at least he'd found a place as an accountant in Grandfather Sullivan's expansive corporation.

Numbers didn't lie. Not like people did.

"Don't you think, Gray?"

His cousin's voice broke into Graham's dismal thoughts. Man, he hated being called Gray. That was his eye color, not his name. "Think what?"

Several of the guys laughed. How much booze had been

imbibed around him? Graham wasn't participating. Not in this bunch, for sure.

"Cadence is lucky to have me. She'd be going nowhere if I hadn't taken pity on her."

Pity? A red haze dimmed Graham's vision. "You don't love her?" Because every woman deserved to be loved, to be cherished by her groom. Especially Cadence Foster.

Graham would cherish her had he been offered half a chance. Okay, he hadn't actually tried. She was so gorgeous, so accomplished, and he'd been — still was — an awkward introvert with few social skills, much to his mother's dismay.

"Love?" Paul shrugged and chuckled. "That's nothing but a bunch of sap. In our circles, it's all about what a marriage contract can bring to the table. All about connections, man." He snapped his fingers, or at least tried to. Several times. Apparently, it wasn't so easy to do for a guy who'd had a few too many.

"It's not sap." Graham's cousin Tate had been married only a couple of weeks ago at the ranch. Tate hadn't known Stephanie long, but he sure hadn't considered what his marriage to a bank-teller-turned-nanny meant to Sullivan Enterprises. The two of them were the most googly-eyed pair Graham had ever seen. Sticky sweet sap at its finest.

Paul's best man, Darrell, cracked open another case of beer and handed cans around. Someone tossed an empty into the pool to raucous laughter. Strident music pounded so fiercely even the strings of solar lights around the patio seemed to shudder in rhythm.

Graham shook his head to clear it. Someone around here needed to keep his wits about him. It had been bad enough thinking of Cadence and Paul together when he thought they loved each other, but now? With Paul proclaiming their upcoming wedding to be basically a business deal?

Was Cadence aware?

Graham's gut soured, and his hands grew clammy as he fisted them. The smog of red anger expanded. The wedding was in only three days. It was going to be a huge affair. The kind of huge that called for ten bridesmaids and ten groomsmen. Hundreds of guests. No expenses spared, because both the Fosters and the Bradleys seemed to have something to prove.

He knew events. Knew numbers. Even so, his mind boggled at the decadence lavished on a party based solely on business and not on love.

"Then don't do it."

Paul's drink was halfway to his mouth when Graham's words seemed to register. He lowered the can slowly as his eyes burned into Graham's. "You're right."

Graham blinked. "I am?"

"My dad and hers have already signed the business side of the deal. I don't have to go through with it."

"Hear, hear!" bellowed one of the groomsmen, saluting with a beer can. Froth overflowed and sloshed down his hand.

"Par-*tay!*" another one yelled.

Graham should walk away now. Groomsman #10 had been present and accounted for. Like he would show up Saturday afternoon, much as it would kill him.

But Paul still stared at him. "She's staying with her parents right now. Do you know where they live?"

Was the guy seriously going to jilt Cadence? Hope bubbled up inside Graham, but it was mingled with horror. Guys didn't simply walk away from a wedding with three days' notice. But then, most guys loved the girl they were going to marry. Didn't they? Graham would. He'd adore the ground she walked on. Especially if she were Cadence Foster.

He managed to clear his throat. "If they're still over on South Elm, yeah."

Paul lifted his beer can as though in toast. "Go tell her it's off."

"You can't do that to her."

"You're the one who talked me into it. Helped me see reason." Paul scowled. "That makes it your job."

Graham rose from the patio chair. "You're a coward. Do it yourself."

"Coward?" Paul lowered his drink to a side table. "You're a number-crunching wuss. You don't have a single muscle in your entire body. You don't get to call me a coward." He slowly rose to his feet, gaze fixed on Graham. The guy's eyes were clear and oh, so, angry. "You'll pay, Gray."

"Pay, Gray!" the best man yelled, and the others joined in the chant.

Graham did so have muscles. Just because he didn't work out the way Paul and his buddies did — uh oh.

"Pool! Pool! Pool!" Darrell switched his tune, and the others followed his cue. They surged toward Graham and, before he knew it, he was flailing high in the air.

Splash!

Graham kicked to the surface of the pool and tread

water. The groomsmen clapped each other on the back, laughing uproariously as they pointed at him.

Paul took a step closer to the edge, still focused on Graham. Would he offer a hand out? Would he apologize for his rowdy friends? Would he say he'd just been kidding, that he was madly in love with Cadence and, of course, he planned to marry her and would treat her like she deserved… a princess?

"You tell her, lover boy." Paul's voice was low and cruel. "If you don't, I'll marry her after all, but I doubt it will last until Christmas. She's kind of needy. You know what I mean?"

Graham swam to the far side and clambered out. He patted the pockets of his shorts. His keys, zipped wallet, and phone were in place. Nothing would likely be damaged from the dunking. He stood, dripping wet, and stared at his cousin across the pool. "You're serious?"

"Never more so."

"Consider it done." Graham turned and strode to the gate separating the courtyard from the roundabout driveway where he'd left his car. His dignified exit sounded like the sham it was as his waterlogged sports sandals slapped against the concrete with every step. At the gate, he turned and looked back.

Only Paul was watching him.

"Last chance to change your mind."

"Do it." Paul turned as Darrell slung his arm across his shoulders. "Bring me the ring."

Graham took a deep breath, let it out slowly, and unlocked his Jetta. See? This was why he should keep his mouth shut. Conversations played out in his head all the time, and their inevitable downward spiral usually provided enough caution to keep Graham's opinions barricaded inside.

No one wanted to hear from him. His workaholic parents certainly never did. He hadn't had close mates in school. The Sullivan cousins he worked with tolerated him at best.

Grandfather's recent purchase of a failing dude ranch in Montana had shocked everyone, though not as much as the reason behind it. Apparently, Grandfather's youthful indiscretions had caught up with him when a daughter he hadn't known existed contacted him. The old man had bought Sweet River Ranch in an effort to integrate two new grandsons in with the five — no, four — who already worked for him. Graham's oldest cousin, Wally, had died in a helicopter crash last fall, leaving a one-year-old in Tate's care.

Why couldn't Graham be more like solid, responsible Tate? What would Tate do with this messy platter Graham had been handed?

Graham slid behind the wheel and pressed the starter. The engine purred to life.

Tate would never have let it get this far. He'd have had the nerve to tell Cadence he loved her long before she'd become engaged to Paul.

The only remaining question was, did Graham go home and change into dry clothes before showing up on Cadence's parents' doorstep? It would add another forty-five minutes, and it was already 9:30.

Best to go now, while he almost had the nerve. Dry clothes wouldn't make things any better.

What on earth had he gotten himself into?

CADENCE FOSTER CHEWED on the end of her pen then tapped it against her leather-bound journal. Shouldn't a woman three days away from her wedding be happier? Mom said everyone got cold feet, and Cadence shouldn't trust her emotions right now.

How about her feelings last week? Last month? Because this sense of impending dread wasn't new. She'd felt all along like something wasn't quite right.

Yes, her marriage to Paul was partly a business deal between their fathers. The Bradleys were considerably wealthier than the Fosters, but Dad had contacts that Paul's father wanted.

But she'd thought she loved Paul — that he loved her — and the business stuff was a sideline, a bonus. Lately, she hadn't been so sure. Paul seemed distant, saying he was busy and had a lot on his mind.

That left her *not* busy... but with a lot on her own mind.

Brides couldn't call off a wedding with only three days' notice. Not when they'd made irreversible decisions like quitting their jobs — Cadence was going to work in Paul's dad's offices after the honeymoon — or moved back home with their parents for the final few weeks. Her roommate had been married recently, and the apartment lease was hers. No problem since Cadence would be moving in with Paul shortly.

She'd burned too many bridges to enable a retreat. There was only one open direction, and that was forward.

Oh, God, please help me!

She didn't dare jot her troubled thoughts into her journal. Not unless she destroyed the thing before Saturday afternoon. If Paul ever read it...

"Honey?" Mom tapped on her bedroom door.

"Yes?"

"There's someone at the door to see you."

Cadence frowned. At nearly ten on a Wednesday evening? "Who is it?"

"Graham Sullivan." Mom clucked disapprovingly. "And he's soaking wet. Doesn't look or sound drunk, though."

Graham? Cadence's heart skipped a beat. Paul's cousin. One of the army of groomsmen Paul had enlisted at Mom's instigation, stretching Cadence's own ability to come up with ten friends to stand up with her.

She remembered Graham as a withdrawn, kind of awkward guy. He'd seemed to have a thing for her once upon a time, but he'd never said anything. It wasn't likely now, either, practically on the eve of her wedding.

"Cadence? He can't possibly have a good reason for being here. I'll send him away."

"I'm coming. I'll talk to him." She tucked her journal in the top drawer and glanced down at herself. Her T-shirt and jogging shorts were decent enough. It was practically bedtime, after all. She opened the door. "Did he say what he wants?"

Mom scowled. "I asked, but he said he wouldn't leave until he talked to you."

The situation was getting stranger by the minute. "Okay."

Mom wrung her hands together. "I don't like this."

"He's harmless."

"If you say so. But still."

"I promise." By now they'd reached the front hall. The glow from the outdoor light fixture shone through the sidelight and illuminated the man on the edge of the landing. He stood with his back to the door and his hands deep in his shorts pockets.

She turned back to her mother. "I'm sure this will only take a minute, but don't worry. Graham's trustworthy."

Mom grimaced as she turned away. "Your father paused our movie, so I'll get back to him. But be careful."

Cadence opened the door, slipped out, and closed it behind her before he turned. "Graham? Mom said you needed to talk to me."

He swallowed hard, his Adam's apple bobbing. "I do."

The words she was going to say to Paul on Saturday evening. If her cold feet didn't get the best of her before then.

"Want to sit down on the patio?" She indicated an alcove a few feet away.

"Um, sure." He gestured. "After you."

He was more of a gentleman than Paul, for all they were cousins. It was their mothers who were sisters, right? She took a seat on the edge of a wicker armchair.

Graham settled into one across from her. "I don't know how to tell you this." His damp sandal poked at a crack in the pavers.

"Spit it out." What could it be? Surely, he hadn't chosen the week of her wedding to dump his undying love at her feet or something else equally corny.

"I came from Paul's bachelor party."

She wrapped her arms around her middle and waited.

"He... sent me to tell you he's calling off the wedding."

Cadence's vision blurred. "He *what?*" Never had she dreamed it would be Paul backing out. In every scenario that ran through her mind, it had been her. She'd give him back the gaudy engagement ring and tell him she didn't love him anymore. Hadn't ever truly loved him. Didn't think she could love him. All those possibilities, but not this one.

"I'm sorry, Cadence. He should have..."

Graham's eyes pleaded with hers, but she wasn't sure what they were saying. "Should have what?"

"Told you himself. Or, better yet, loved you like you deserve to be loved." Then he shook his head and looked down.

Maybe Graham did care. Maybe she hadn't imagined it all those years ago. Too bad he hadn't been more candid then. But would she have given him a real chance? She doubted it. Paul was flashier. Way more fun.

Also, she might have been stupid and immature.

She *knew* she had been.

Cadence twisted the ring on her finger and slowly tugged it off. "What did his royal highness say to do with this?"

"I'll return it to him, unless you want to do it yourself."

Did she? There'd be some satisfaction in giving him a piece of her mind, but did she actually want to see him, talk to him, give him a chance to tell her he hadn't meant it and, of course, he wanted to marry her on Saturday? That this was some sort of joke? The group of friends he'd been coaching to be groomsmen might have egged him on, especially if alcohol had been flowing.

She studied Graham, who sat a few feet away from her, leaning on his elbows, looking down. The man's T-shirt clung to his shoulders. His damp board shorts stuck to his thighs. "Why are you wet?"

"They threw me in the pool."

"Because?"

Graham scratched his neck. Stared down at the pavers. "I might have called Paul a coward."

Cadence wasn't sure whether it was sobs or laughter surging out of her, but it was all just too much.

CHAPTER TWO

She thought it was funny?

Graham lifted his gaze to the woman seated across from him. She howled with laughter... and all at the thought Paul's minions had tossed him in the pool. He'd felt so sorry for her that he'd come straight here, regardless of his personal discomfort, and she laughed?

Wait a sec.

Those gales sounded mighty on edge. And now mingled with sobs. Aw, man. What did a guy do with a hysterical woman? This was far worse than one who laughed at his personal plight.

He was an only child, and his mother showed so little emotion he'd had no experience dealing with it. Toss in a bunch of guy cousins, and... what was he supposed to do with Cadence now? Had he expected her to nod, square her shoulders, and carry on?

Fat chance. He'd get to dry off, exchange his chlorine-coated contacts for his glasses, and forget this ever happened, but her life's plans had derailed, never to follow the same trajectory again. Of course, the situation was traumatic.

"Cadence?"

"What?" She hiccupped as she looked at him, tears streaming down her face.

Tears. She'd brought out the big guns.

Graham scrubbed the back of his neck, where his short hair was already dry. "Is there anything I can do for you?" Oh, wasn't he full of helpful words tonight.

She snorted something between a shocked laugh and a cry. "Not unless you can conjure up a job and an apartment." She snapped her fingers. "Preferably far away from anyone who's going to laugh or offer false sympathy. I can't believe this. I bet everyone saw it coming except me. He got what he wanted most with that deal with my dad. He didn't ever even w-w-want me."

Cadence's jaw trembled as she looked down. Then her long, dark hair cascaded in front of her face, hiding her expression.

How could he just sit there and watch someone going through heartbreak as though it were a clinical observation? He couldn't. Graham crouched beside her chair and ran his hand lightly over her heaving shoulders.

He caught his breath at the sensation of her T-shirt beneath his fingers. The fragrant floral scent of her. Graham steeled himself. He'd thought he was over his crush on her — it had been years since he'd allowed his indulgent thoughts free rein — but tonight crashed the gates wide open again.

"You don't have a job?"

She laughed, a bitter sound. "I quit mine because I was going to work for Paul's dad after the honeymoon."

He wasn't going to think about her and Paul on a honeymoon. It was off. "And a place to live?" But wouldn't it be the same answer?

"My roommate got married a couple of weeks ago. It was her lease, and of course, she wanted to share the place with her husband, not me. That was fine. I didn't need it. I was—"

"You were moving in with Paul." He sighed.

"Yeah. So, I've been here—" she waved a hand toward the stately house "—for the interim. My stuff is in boxes in the garage."

She really was at an impasse. "I... I might have a solution."

Shut up, Graham. It's a terrible idea given your crush.

No, you *shut up.*

"What do you mean?" A glimmer of hope entered her voice.

If he were like Tate, he'd offer to elope with her on the spot. Gallant, confident Tate.

Graham was not like Tate. But maybe... maybe all was not lost. "I've been in Montana for the past few months."

Confusion clouded her brow.

Touching her wasn't helping. He backed up into his chair again and met her gaze. "It's a long story, but my Grandfather Sullivan bought a failing dude ranch out there and summoned all of us to turn it around."

"I see?"

She didn't see.

"My cousin Tate... you remember him?"

15

Cadence nodded.

"He's acting as Chief Operating Officer, and Grandfather assigned me CFO."

"Chief Financial Officer."

Graham nodded. "So, I… uh, I happen to know we have job vacancies. We also have available staff housing, partly furnished."

"You're offering me a job? On a ranch in Montana?" Disbelief colored her voice.

"Yeah, sorry. It's all I can think of. I flew west in April at Grandfather's command, but I'm planning on driving back next week. It's been a pain not having my car there, even though there's no place to go. Jewel Lake is about a half hour out, and I can catch a ride to church with one of the cousins, but sometimes a guy needs…" He cut off his rambling in mid-sentence.

She stared at him. "A dude ranch?"

"I know. It's the last place I expected to land up, myself. Grandfather says it will take two or three years, but I'm hoping to come back to Chicago by fall and do the ranch books remotely."

"A ranch."

Hadn't he said that like five times? "Yes, but I work in the office. It's a full resort with cabin rentals and an RV park and a lodge. People can ride horses or take kayaks out on the little lake or go hiking or fishing." The thought of all that outdoorsiness made him shudder.

"I love riding."

Graham blinked. "You ride? Horseback?"

"Summer camp. I lived for the horses."

"Oh. Well. That's great then." He studied her face in the glow of the solar lights. Was she considering…?

"Are you serious? About the offer, I mean."

No. He was absolutely crazy to encourage her. She'd be nearby, and she'd find some other guy, like maybe his cousin Bryce, and Graham would have to watch it unfold yet again. On the other hand, he couldn't simply walk away and make her deal with the fallout of a wedding cancelled at the last minute when she was at the end of her own resources. Not when he could offer her a way out. "Uh, yes?"

"When next week? No. Even Monday is too late." She bit her lip. "Tomorrow? Early?"

Graham opened his mouth to protest but shut it again. The only reason he was in the city at all was this wedding that wasn't going to happen. He'd drop the ring back to Paul, return to his apartment, pack up his stuff, catch a few winks, swing by for Cadence, and hit the road.

Why not?

Because it was a really, really bad idea, that was why not. On the other hand, it might be the best idea he'd ever had.

God? What do You say?

The heavens did not part. There was no holy, booming voice. Not even a still, small whisper.

He was on his own here. And all he could think of was Cadence, bravely facing this mess alone.

Before he'd consciously decided to go for it, he found himself nodding. "Let's exchange contact info, and I'll text you when I'm ready to roll. The Jetta has a reasonable amount of cargo space, but you'll need to pick what's most important for the summer. I hope you'll plan to stay at least through Labor Day if we give you a job."

"Sounds good. I understand." Cadence unlocked her phone, poked around in it then held it out to him.

Ah, she'd opened it to 'add contact.' Graham tapped his info in and hit 'save' before glancing up. "I can't promise your perfect job. I… I don't even know what you do." He'd tried so hard to avoid thinking about her over the past few years.

"I've been a social media marketer for Lake Effect."

One of the premier local tourism sites? Graham nearly dropped her phone. "Seriously?" He managed to hand it back without incident.

"Why would I lie?" She tapped into her cell.

His pinged with an incoming text. He glanced at it. Cadence had said hi, so now he had her number. "I didn't mean it that way. It's just… social media is one of our big needs at Sweet River Ranch right now."

"Then I'm your girl."

If only that were true.

CADENCE AVOIDED HER PARENTS' wing of the house as she padded toward the garage to examine her pile of belongings. How big was Graham's car? He'd said the staff housing was partially furnished, but what did that mean?

She shifted a few boxes of Christmas ornaments and winter clothes to one side and eyed what remained. She wouldn't need five boxes of paperbacks, but she hadn't packed with the thought of sorting them. Everyday clothes, obviously. Her honeymoon bags stacked in her bedroom had been filled for a tropical vacation. None of that was relevant. From upstairs, all she needed were her purse and personal care items.

Cadence moved six boxes toward the garage door then stacked the book boxes behind them in case there was room. The rest could stay. She'd get Mom to ship things if she'd miscalculated.

Mom.

Cadence wrapped her arms around herself. Her parents were going to be devastated, possibly even angry. They'd sunk a ton of money into this wedding and, with the tight timeline, they'd lose much of it. Could they absorb the losses? As far as Cadence knew, they could, but still. It wasn't fair to make them do that.

Should she see if they were still awake and explain things? They'd try to talk her into patching things up with Paul. Mom, especially, adored the guy, gushing about him constantly.

How did Cadence know Graham was telling the truth? Maybe he'd made the whole thing up. She replayed their conversation but couldn't see that as a likely path. If she truly loved Paul, she'd drive over to his place right now and beg him to reconsider.

She didn't love him that much. Possibly not at all. The wedding had seemed like a good idea last year when he'd proposed, but the chemistry was all wrong. Why had she said yes? Right, he'd proposed in a big way in front of all their friends. She'd been thrilled. She'd also been stupid.

And now a lifeline had appeared. There was no begging Paul for a redo. She didn't want one. This was relief all the way... except for the embarrassment. Oh, and the lack of a job and place to live.

Graham offered answers to every piece of that.

She was on her way to Montana, running off like a 'fraidy-cat, leaving others to face the music and pick up the pieces. She tiptoed quietly through the house and pulled out a piece of paper. Time to write a letter to her parents.

That took a while. Two sheets were crumpled in the trash before she was reasonably satisfied.

Her phone pinged. Graham had texted.

I gave Paul the ring.

Thanks.

She drummed her fingers on the desk before deciding.

I don't think I can sleep tonight.

Me either.

Want to hit the road? I'm happy to drive for the first few hours if you're tired.

Now?

Duh. Of course, now.

Why not? I wrote a letter to leave for my folks.

Won't they notice if I drive in?

She was winning.

> I'll disarm the alarm and reset it when we leave.

> Are you sure?

> Absolutely.

> I'll be there in a little more than an hour. I'll text you when I'm leaving the apartment. Bring food.

Such a guy. She grinned and pumped her fist.

> Will do. I'll be waiting for you. I've sorted my boxes.

> Sounds good. See you soon.

Cadence looked around her childhood bedroom. She had time for a shower and then she'd take what she needed down to the garage and wait for Graham there.

Was she really doing this? Running away from all her problems, just like that?

Paul had done it first. He was the jerk, not her, but her parents might not see it that way.

Cadence bit her lip. She'd text her girlfriends — her bridesmaids — tomorrow while Graham was driving. How far was it to Montana, anyway? Where was Jewel Lake? She'd never heard of it.

A quick search on her phone brought up the small town's website. It was on the other side of the Rocky

Mountain divide, near Missoula. It looked like a great little place tucked amid rolling hills and ranch land.

Ranch land. What was the name of the ranch he'd mentioned? Sweet River.

Another search brought up a website. She cringed. So basic. Yes, there were a few photos of a log lodge and some cottages by a lake. More like a puddle, compared to Lake Michigan. But if the ranch had any social media accounts, they weren't evident from the main page. And they should be.

Cadence cracked her knuckles. Graham wasn't making all this up. They did need her, and she'd do the best she could for them.

It wasn't every day that a woman met an angel in disguise, but that's what Graham Sullivan was.

Yeah, she knew he was a regular guy. Their circles had intersected slightly during college.

But tonight, and for the foreseeable future, he was her angel.

Did believing in angels mean she believed in God? She'd never quite stopped, but the Almighty hadn't seemed all that relevant in recent years. She hadn't been asking for His guidance or anything like that.

Maybe she should have been. It might have saved her a whole lot of trouble, not to mention humiliation.

Well, she'd pray now and thank God for Graham. And maybe she'd seek His advice over the next while.

CHAPTER THREE

Cadence's cell trilled for the umpteenth time.

Graham glanced over. This time, she stirred a little in the passenger seat, blinking sleepily as she became aware of her surroundings.

He clenched the steering wheel and forced his gaze forward through the car's windshield. He'd been sneaking peeks at her since he'd taken over driving somewhere in mid-Wisconsin.

She was adorable, even in sleep.

And she was not his. She was not in a position to be his.

The phone stopped ringing, then beeped as it recorded a voicemail, also not for the first time.

Cadence gathered her dark hair and pushed it over her shoulder as she looked around. "Where are we?"

"West of Rochester."

"Minnesota?"

He chuckled. "Definitely not New York."

"But we've been driving for—" She looked at the dash clock.

"Five and a half hours." They hadn't left Chicago until 2:30, not that stopping off to give Paul the engagement ring had taken long. Paul and the guys had consumed a lot of alcohol in the couple of hours Graham had been gone, and abusive cursing seemed their preferred language. He'd gotten out of there as quickly as he could, thankful he hadn't endured another toss in the pool.

And then it had taken a bit of time to close up his apartment again. He'd planned to haul a full carload to Montana but limited himself to the carryon he'd brought on the plane as well as a small cooler with the measly contents of his fridge. No doubt, Cadence would fill every remaining nook and cranny of the Jetta.

He'd been right about that. The trunk was packed to the gills, and the backseat stuffed to the ceiling. Also, he was dying to know what books she liked to read that took up three of those boxes. She'd been reluctant to leave any behind, but the car was only so big.

Her phone trilled again.

Cadence closed her eyes then turned it face-up listlessly and stared at it. "My mother."

"It's rung a few times." Like eight in the past half hour because, yes, he'd been counting.

"I guess I should answer."

Graham bit his tongue and passed a semi-truck.

She sighed heavily. "Hi, Mom."

He couldn't make out Mrs. Foster's exact response, but the shrill volume came through loud and clear. A quick glance revealed Cadence leaning against the headrest with her eyes closed, absorbing the tirade.

"I'm sorry, Mom. I'll pay you back."

More high-pitched screeching.

"No, I know I can't reimburse you for the embarrassment. Canceling wasn't my idea. Did I forget to tell you it was Paul who asked for the ring back?"

Graham doubted she hadn't mentioned it in the note she said she'd left, but her words still soured in his stomach. She would have married Paul in two days if last night hadn't happened.

He needed to keep that in mind. He might have admired her from afar for years, but she wasn't free. Not really.

Maybe in a few months.

Stop it, Graham. She'll never see anything in a geek like you. She didn't before, and she won't now.

Would it kill him to dream?

It might.

"No, Mom. I won't change my mind. I'm not running after Paul Bradley and begging him to marry me after all. How desperate and wrong would that be?"

Very desperate. Very wrong.

"Think how your father feels."

Ah, finally Mrs. Foster had calmed enough that her voice came through as something definable rather than a high-pitched wa-wa-wa from a Charlie Brown cartoon.

"Tell Dad I'm sorry it worked out like this, but I have to go now. We're approaching a gas station, and I need the facilities." Cadence gave Graham a pleading look.

They'd switched drivers at the side of the road hours ago. No doubt she needed a restroom. So did he. Also, breakfast would not go amiss.

"Bye, Mom. Yes, I'll keep in touch. I'm sorry. Again." She

tapped to end the call and dropped her phone onto her lap. "Oh, man. Have you ever disappointed your parents as much as I just did?"

Graham couldn't help the chuckle. "By being a guy who loves numbers and books instead of sports and clubs? I've been disappointing them since I was born."

Cadence angled her head and studied him. "You don't think they approve of you?"

"Nope. Not really." He signaled for the off-ramp into Kasson. "Let's fuel up and get breakfast."

"I'll pay." She fumbled for the purse at her feet.

"I've got it."

"But—"

Graham set his hand over hers. His heart jolted, and he pulled away quickly. "I was going to drive to Montana, anyway."

"You weren't expecting a stowaway."

"True, but I've got it. Okay?"

Her lips tightened. "Fine. This time."

It was a small victory. He couldn't truly take care of her the way he dreamed of, but he could do it in small ways. Ways like offering her a job — he ought to call Grandfather about that, or maybe Tate — and a place to live and transportation. Fine. He was doing a lot. All he could. He'd do the same for anyone caught in a predicament like hers.

Maybe not. Maybe his generosity was all because of Cadence Foster.

Graham took in the small town. "There's a restaurant. Let's get breakfast."

She turned luminescent eyes toward him. "After that, I

guess I'd better start calling my bridesmaids. I can't believe what a tangled mess this all is."

"Fortification first." He pulled into the parking lot and cut the engine. "It's going to be a hard couple of days for you."

Cadence pushed the car door open and climbed out as he did the same. "How much further to the ranch?" she asked him overtop the car.

Graham laughed. "It's about a twenty-four-hour drive, total. And we're less than six in. We'll be a while."

Her eyes bugged. "That far?"

"Yes, ma'am."

"Oh. My. Goodness. I didn't realize."

"It's a big country. Let me remind you — you said you wanted to get far, far away."

"I did, but wow." She shook her head lightly as she straightened. "Okay. Breakfast. I'm starving."

"Me, too."

It was quite a while later before her group text with her ten would-be bridesmaids finally quieted enough for Cadence to set her phone down. She glanced over at Graham. "Sorry I've been such lousy company."

He flashed her a grin. "No problem. We're now in North Dakota."

She peered out the window. "It doesn't look any different from Minnesota."

Graham chuckled.

Cadence angled a look at him, but he seemed focused

out the windshield. Which gave her a chance to take a closer look. After all, she owed him a lot and, besides twenty-four hours in a car together, she'd be working with him. Or, at least, his family.

Hopefully him.

What was that reaction about? She narrowed her gaze and took in his profile. She'd never truly noticed him before. He was the quiet, unassuming cousin trapped between the Bradley side of his family — Paul was definitely *not* inconspicuous — and the Sullivans with their four outgoing sons.

He was cute. She could get used to seeing his face, even in the glasses he sported today. His dark hair was shorter on the sides than on the top. It looked like he'd gotten a fresh cut for the wedding.

Graham glanced over and caught her staring. His cheeks pinked.

Oh, boy. She was honestly scrutinizing him in that way. Cadence cleared her throat. "So, tell me more about our destination and what I'll be doing."

"I haven't called anyone yet." He frowned as though he were nervous. "As far as I know, the social media manager job is still open. We also need a photographer—"

She did a mental fist-pump. "You definitely do. I looked up the website."

"And if, by some chance, Tate hired someone in the past three days and forgot to tell me, there are plenty of other openings. The gift shop. Housekeepers. Horse… people."

"Stable hands? Muck shovelers?"

"Whatever they do."

Cadence couldn't help laughing at him. "Have you been

riding since you moved out there? I bet the trails are beautiful."

"Once." Graham grimaced. "There were mosquitoes. Also, Tate brought his girlfriend — now his wife — so I was a total third wheel."

"Poor you. Wait! Did you say Tate is married? When did that happen?" And how had her social contacts failed to inform her? Not that she knew the family well, but they did run in the same general circles. Surely, someone should have informed her.

"It was a bit of a surprise." Graham let out a long breath. "Okay, we have time for a story. Have you met my grandfather?"

Cadence blinked. If they were starting with the Sullivan patriarch, the tale could be long. "Walter Sullivan? I've met him, but I doubt he'd remember me."

"I bet he would."

"I'm not that memorable."

Graham's eyebrows angled above his dark-rimmed glasses when he looked at her.

Didn't he believe her? Hmm.

"He doesn't forget anyone or anything. I've seen no sign of that slipping even now that he's eighty." He pursed his lips. "Though I did wonder back in April."

She nestled deeper into the leather seat. "What happened then?"

"He summoned my cousins and me to Montana to see this ranch he'd bought. I thought he'd lost his marbles. Sullivan does hotels, not dude ranches. We all thought we'd be spending a few days together — maybe a week or two — and then return to Chicago, doing what we do best."

For him, that would be crunching numbers, right? Sounded boring, but someone needed to do it to keep the universe rotating. So long as it wasn't her.

"But then we found out why he'd bought the ranch. Seems like he'd had an affair with his office secretary way back before he met our grandmother. The woman quit working for him, and after a while, he forgot all about her. Until January when his daughter showed up in his office with DNA proof of their relationship."

"Wait, what?"

"Yep. And his daughter — whom I have a hard time calling my aunt — has two sons." He heaved a sigh. "It's not that I want Weston and Jude for cousins, but maybe they're an upgrade over Paul."

Cadence snorted. Oops, not so ladylike. "It doesn't take much to be an improvement."

"Right now, I'd have to agree with you." Graham shook his head. "Anyway, Grandfather bought the ranch, which someone had started to turn into a resort — a guest ranch — but then run out of money. He decided it would be a great way to get everyone to know each other as we work together to pull that property into the black."

"Huh. That's interesting. It's hard to believe that about your grandfather, though. He's always seemed very... controlled."

"I guess he was young once. Not that it excuses him."

"So, will it be possible to make Sweet River profitable?"

"Oh, yeah. He's throwing enough money at it, but he doesn't care about that. With a solid foundation, it will pay the company back. Eventually."

"What do you like best about living there?"

His lip curled as he glanced at her. "Not much."

Cadence laughed. "Oh, come on. It can't be that bad."

"I'm not so fond of horses and bugs. I prefer more luxury in my accommodations, but my new aunt is the lodge chef, and she's a good cook, so I guess that's a plus." He shrugged. "I have lots of time to read?"

That caught her attention. "You're a reader? What's your favorite genre?"

"Thrillers."

"Ugh, not me."

"So those boxes of books — there's nothing in there for me to borrow? I should have made you leave them in your parents' garage."

"You're very funny."

He smirked but didn't turn her direction.

"You're probably too busy doing all the stuff at the ranch to read, anyway."

Graham shuddered. "Well, I'm getting along better with my cousins than I used to — Tate, at least — so I guess that's good."

"Tate always seemed pretty easy-going to me? Again, not that I know him well."

"Yeah, I guess. We never really connected, even though we're the same age, but now we're in the same office — along with our grandfather — and we're doing okay."

"I was sorry to hear of Wally's death last fall. That must have been rough on everyone."

Graham's fingers flexed on the wheel. "It didn't affect me much at the time, since we weren't close, but I did feel bad for their family. Wally and his wife left a little boy. Tate is Jamie's guardian. Well, Tate and now his wife, Stephanie."

She tried to place the remaining Sullivan brothers. "Are Bryce and Maxwell in Montana, too?"

"Yes. They're working with Jude on maintenance and grounds and renovations and all that stuff. Weston — the other new relative — is an actual cowboy. He's in charge of the stables."

"Are they nice?"

The look Graham shot her said otherwise. He sighed deeply before adding words. "Jude's quiet. He's okay, I guess. Weston has a chip on his shoulder and is always snarking around like he has something to prove."

"Sounds fun." Not.

"But there are a few dozen people working there now. Quite a few women. You shouldn't have any trouble making friends."

Did she want new friends? After that barrage of texts earlier today from the ones she was leaving behind, she wasn't entirely sure she was in the market to replace them. Life might be a whole lot quieter without as much input.

Lonelier, too, probably. Could she survive ranch life after the bustling city? For the summer, she'd manage, unless Graham's grandfather fired her even before he hired her.

Maybe lonelier and quieter wasn't an all-bad thing.

"Want me to drive?"

"Sure. I'll pull off at the next exit. Then I guess I'd better call Tate and make sure I haven't brought you on a wild goose chase."

CHAPTER FOUR

Tate looked up from his laptop, leaned back, and crossed his arms when Graham staggered into the office the next morning. "Tell me more. When did you get in?"

"An hour ago."

Tate's eyebrows angled up. "You drove through the night?"

"Mostly. We left Chicago at something like two a.m. and swapped driving every few hours." Didn't that make it two nights on the road? The details were blurring.

Tate waited.

"If I'd been thinking that through... I mean, I know it's roughly a 24-hour drive, so obviously we'd arrive in the middle of the night. But I didn't think about that at the time. Solo, I'd have started at a sane time of day, found a hotel at midpoint, and arrived here in the evening." He'd have been rested, which was definitely not the case now.

"You could have stopped anyway. Or did you?"

Graham sighed. "We pulled off at a rest area and tried

to sleep for a few hours, but tons of semi-trucks blasted past, plus it was impossible to get comfortable. Cadence brought so much stuff we couldn't even tilt the seats back."

Tate snorted, glee dancing in his eyes.

What was so funny? Graham couldn't see the joke, not that he was at his brightest after the long journey. Even the quick shower he'd grabbed at his place before leaving Cadence there to nap hadn't helped. Nor had the coffee he'd snagged from the lodge kitchen on his way into the office.

Tate snickered. "You went to Chicago for your cousin's wedding. You *rescued*—" he air-quoted the word "—a jilted bride, offered her a job, and drove straight back several days early. What happened to the Graham Sullivan I've known all my life?"

Graham took a sip of life-giving brew. Hopefully also head-clearing. "It's a long story."

"I've got nothing but time."

He laughed. "So not true. Doesn't Grandfather have a list a mile long for you to do before you head to Chicago yourself?" Tate was taking Stephanie and Jamie on this trip to wrap up negotiations with Chester Hotels. They'd also be attending the Gala of the Stars on Independence Day. Graham had made an appearance a few times, and it was not one of the events he would miss. Too many people. Too pretentious.

"Of course." Tate smirked. "But he won't be in the office for another half hour. He's in a meeting with Nadine and the kitchen crew."

Aunt Nadine. Not that Graham could bring himself to use the title any more than Tate could. "You probably don't require more information than I already gave you. Cadence needed a place to go until all this dies down. She's a photographer and a social media expert. We need those skills here at Sweet River. Bam. Done."

Tate chuckled and shook his head. "Do you have a thing for her?"

Graham narrowed his gaze. "You're one to talk, hiring Stephanie to be Jamie's nanny when you barely knew her but couldn't keep your eyes off of her."

"So, you *are* attracted to Cadence Foster."

"I briefly was, back five or eight years ago. But that's definitely not why she's here."

"Convince me."

"What does it matter? We have an opening that matches her skills. We have vacant staff housing or, at least, we did last week. Is it full?"

"Mostly, but we can do some rearranging."

"What's the problem? Set a time for an interview if you want to be more formal. You'll soon see she's perfect."

His cousin scrutinized him.

"For the job, cuz. Yeah, I maybe had a crush on her a long time ago, but you'd have rescued her, too, under the circumstances. You wouldn't have left her within reach of Paul and that whole fiasco, either. Even if you are married to Stephanie now. My offer to Cadence wasn't anything personal."

"Paul Bradley's a moron."

"Agreed. I can't believe he dumped her three days before the wedding. Then he called Cadence a dozen times yesterday while we were driving, begging her to come back, that he hadn't meant to do it. She finally blocked his number."

"Only you." Tate's muttered words were so low, Graham barely heard them.

But he did. "What was that supposed to mean?"

"Who but a softie like you would go to a wedding and help the bride run away?"

Graham set the coffee cup down carefully, so he could cross his arms and widen his stance without spilling anything. "You make it sound like I'm trying to scoop up women wherever I go and by whatever means possible. I haven't even dated in years."

Tate hadn't either, before Stephanie. It got so complicated. Most of the people in their circles weren't believers. They ricocheted from one relationship to the next without thinking anything of it. Divorce was as common as marriage. So long as money kept flowing, no one seemed to care a whole lot. And the women not in their circles? Mostly saw the dollar signs attached to the Sullivan name.

It was hard. Some would say it was cry-me-a-river hard, because didn't money count for a lot? It helped, for sure. But it didn't make relationships easy one tiny speck.

Tate glanced at his watch. "Grandfather and I will meet with her at 11:00 if that's fine. You're welcome to sit in."

"I'll let her know, but I'll leave the three of you to it. She doesn't need me lurking."

A tiny smirk hovered at the corners of Tate's mouth. "Your call. Where is she now?"

"At my place, but she needs a place to live."

"I'll handle it."

Graham held up both hands, palms out. "No problem. I

know I booked this whole week off, but I'm here now, so I'll catch up on some paperwork this morning." He snagged his coffee cup and pointed it toward his cubicle. Maybe someday Grandfather would have proper offices built in the lodge.

Maybe Graham didn't care, since he wasn't needed in Montana as much as the hands-on crews. He could work remotely from his apartment or from the Sullivan building in Chicago. Numbers didn't care where they were crunched from.

Although it was kind of nice not being around the Paul Bradley types every day. Not having the hum of traffic underlying every moment. Hearing the calls of loons on the little lake was a pleasant change from the wails of sirens.

He shook his head as he made his way to the cubicle. Did he think he was going to turn into a country bumpkin like Weston or Jude? Fat chance.

Although country gentleman had a much nicer ring to it.

First, he'd shoot Cadence a text to tell her when to be ready for him to pick her up for her interview. Then he'd find some numbers to align.

Numbers were good. Unemotional. They did what they were told, every single time.

Not like humans.

WALTER SULLIVAN FOLDED his hands on his desk and looked at her with hawklike eyes. "You're hired."

"Thank you, sir. I'm grateful for this opportunity, and you won't regret it."

"Tate, can we partition off another area of this room?"

Cadence's gaze bounced over to the unlit corner, which was apparently Graham's space, though he was out at the moment. She'd work in the same office as him and the other top brass? Although, she could see there weren't many other options in the lodge's wings.

Tate tapped his jaw as he slowly took in the room. "I think so. I'll message Heather to see what she can figure out."

"I'll be out a lot with the photography stuff, right? And to most events so I can post them on social media? I might not even need an office. I can probably work from staff housing, if the internet is decent there."

Walter eliminated her comments with one sweep of his hand. "You need an office."

"Okay. Thank you."

"Staff quarters are nearly filled up." Tate studied his screen. "I think I'll have to put you with Paisley Teele. She's in a two-bedroom. She's nice — she works in activities programming. I wish I could offer you your own place, but it's not the reality right now."

Cadence bit her lip. "I appreciate whatever you can do." It was even true, but honestly? Graham's half-duplex had two bedrooms, and the whole thing was tiny. She'd be sharing that square footage with a stranger... and she'd just promised to stay for at least ten weeks, through the busy summer season.

"The staff-housing units are small." Tate winced. "I know it."

Didn't he have an expansive penthouse in Chicago? Paul had mocked it to her once. Why had she stuck with that poser as long as she had? Agreed to marry him? Man, she'd had a close call, and the repercussions of the breakup were far from over. The wedding was to have been tomorrow, and Mom was still calling every couple of hours with yet another panic attack as she begged Cadence to catch the next flight home.

Cadence felt bad. She did. The salary she'd be making here at Sweet River Ranch wasn't going to make a dent in her debt to her parents anytime soon, but she'd chip away at it. Thankfully, the Bradleys had handled some of the expenses, like the reception at their country club. Paul could deal with the fall-out from that end of things.

Maybe she could find some freelance work as well. A ranch resort couldn't possibly fill her time like a busy life in the city had. Being single again would give her more free time than she'd had while planning a wedding. Although Mom had done most of that.

Tate's fingers still danced over his keyboard. "I'm adding you to the staff meals roster for the dining room. In fact, lunch is ready shortly. I'd take you over and introduce you to Nadine, but I'm headed for the airport as soon as I wrap this up."

"Graham said he'd meet me when I'm done here."

The guy smirked. "Sure. Graham can show you around. Get him to introduce you to Paisley." Tate gestured to the door as he rose. "After you, Cadence. And welcome to the motley crew at Sweet River."

"Thank you." She pulled the door open to find Graham

lounging against the wall, poking at something on his phone.

He looked up. Grinned. Slid his phone into his pocket. "How did it go?" Then his gaze seemed to catch on his cousin behind her.

If Tate hadn't been there watching, Cadence might have thrown her arms around Graham and thanked him profusely for everything he'd done for her. Simply a gesture of gratitude, of course, but Tate might slant it wrong. He'd seemed mildly amused throughout the entire interview.

"You're looking at Sweet River's newest hire."

"Congratulations." Graham looked past her to Tate. "Thanks."

"You're welcome. She'll be a good fit."

The lunch bell chimed, and Graham angled his head toward the common area. "Let me introduce you around the dining room."

Much as Cadence tried to ignore Tate following them, she could feel his presence until he veered toward the main lodge doors. Whew. She leaned closer to Graham. "I'm supposed to meet Paisley." Was that even a real name? "I hear I'll be rooming with her."

Graham frowned. "I didn't think we were to the doubling-up stage."

Maybe not for the Sullivan grandsons, but Cadence wasn't on the same level at Sweet River. She hadn't been in Chicago, either.

The dining room was a happening place. Families and groups crowded around over half of the tables, while many more stood in a cafeteria line, chatting and laughing with each other. A middle-aged woman and two younger ones stood on the other side of the counter helping people with their food selections.

"What's for lunch?" Cadence asked Graham. "Smells good."

He directed her attention to the chalkboard with the day's meals listed. "Taco salad, looks like. I hope they have refried beans. It's not a real taco salad without."

When he leaned close to her like that, he emitted evergreen and musk, like an outdoorsy guy should smell. Cadence doubted he thought of himself as outdoorsy, though. He'd shuddered at the thought of horseback riding, but there were plenty of other ways to enjoy nature, and this ranch seemed full of options.

Oooh! She could take out a kayak or go for a hike or ride a horse anytime at all, upload images — selfies or not — hashtag them with #SweetRiverRanch, and she'd be doing actual work. This might be the best summer ever.

Graham leaned in close again. "That woman over there talking to those kids, wearing a plaid shirt and jean shorts? That's Paisley."

Cadence studied her roommate-to-be, who had a broad smile as she chatted with a couple of tweens. The kids lapped up her attention. "She looks friendly."

Graham sighed. "So *very* friendly."

She smirked back at him. "Does she have designs on you?" The thought of having a front-row seat to her roommate's romance with the guy who'd rescued her was amusing. Unsettling, but amusing.

"I hope not. I don't think she's noticed me. She's super

outgoing and chatty with everyone. It's... exhausting. I hope you'll be okay with her."

"I'm sure I will." It wasn't like she'd been offered any choices. "Friendly people are much nicer to be around than grumpy ones. Like that cowboy over there." She poked her chin toward a guy glowering around the room.

Graham snorted quietly. "My newfound cousin Weston, the horse wrangler. I don't get him. He seems to judge everything around him as sardonically amusing, if worthy of any attention at all."

"He must have been hurt in his past life."

"What?" Graham drew back a little. "What do you mean? I think he's naturally a jerk."

They shifted forward in the food line. "Not usually. People who hold back and don't connect with others easily have usually suffered some sort of relationship trauma."

His eyebrows rose a little. "Now you're scaring me."

"How so?"

"You analyze everyone, and I'm starting to worry how you see me."

Something flickered inside her, but she squelched it. "I see you as a genuinely nice guy who can't stand by when someone is hurting. You jump in to help, even when there's nothing in it for you."

Graham's Adam's apple bobbed as he searched her eyes for a few seconds then looked away.

Wait. Was that a flush on his cheeks? Did he have hopes that something might come out of rescuing her? She was in no position to give him any hope. She needed time to heal.

Tomorrow should have been her wedding.

But all she could feel was an overwhelming sense of

relief that she would not become Cadence Bradley. She'd been offered a new direction in life, and she was going to embrace it to the fullest.

Bring on Sweet River Ranch. Bring on a bubbly, smiley, chatty roommate.

Bring on Graham Sullivan.

She had this.

CHAPTER FIVE

P aisley?"

Aw, the guy sounded so nervous that it was nearly endearing. Cadence stood beside Graham, waiting for the other woman to wrap her conversation and turn their way.

Finally, she turned and looked between them with her sparkling green eyes. "Hi! It's Graham, isn't it?"

"Yes." He swallowed so hard Cadence could hear it. "This is Cadence Foster. She's just joined us from Chicago, and she's taking on the photographer and social media position."

"I'm so happy to meet you! You're going to love it here." Paisley's smile widened.

Cadence couldn't remember the last time a total stranger had been so excited to meet her. "Thank you," she murmured, shaking Paisley's hand. Then she backed up a step in case this woman was headed in for an embrace. Paisley looked like a hugger.

"As you may know, staff housing is close to capacity,

and we're now to the doubling-up stage. Tate has assigned Cadence to be your roommate." Graham hesitated a beat. "I hope that's okay."

"More than okay! It will be so much fun to have a roommate. I'll have to rein in all my stuff, though. I'm sort of spread out all over, but it won't take long to clear out the loft. I hope you don't mind that I've got the main floor bedroom? Oh, you probably have no idea what I'm talking about!"

"I've been inside Graham's place." Hopefully, that wasn't admitting something she shouldn't. "If they're all the same layout, the loft is fine."

After all, beggars couldn't be choosers. Maybe she could find a curtain to help with privacy, since the lofts were open to the minuscule living room below.

"That's excellent!"

Did she always speak in exclamation points? Was Cadence up for ten weeks of Paisley Teele? But it would sure beat living with an angry, grumpy person. It would sure beat living with Paul Bradley. Being married to him.

Cadence suppressed a shudder.

"I've got a riding lesson with several tweens at one." Paisley checked her watch. "But I'll be free for a bit at three. I'd say to go ahead without me, but I wasn't kidding about my stuff having exploded all over the place. Can I meet you there at three or four?"

Graham touched the small of Cadence's back as he nodded at Paisley. "That will be fine. Her belongings are all in my car at the moment. You're in unit six, right?"

Paisley nodded. "That's right. Oh, I'm so excited! I can

hardly wait to get to know you. We're going to be best friends. I know it."

Cadence held her smile in place. "I hope so." But she wasn't quite as sure as Paisley seemed to be.

Also, she was a little distracted by the gentle pressure on her back. Had Paul ever touched her like that? He must have, but he'd been much more forward. More brash. Less with the polite niceties.

"The lunch line is nearly through," Graham said. "Ready, Cadence? Paisley, have you—"

"I've eaten! Catch you two later." Paisley fluttered her fingertips and twirled away.

Cadence let out a breath. "Is she for real?"

"Do you want me to ask Tate if there are any other options?" Graham studied her.

No glasses blocked her view of his gorgeous gray eyes today. "No. It will be fine, I'm sure. But she is a bit much. I have a sneaking suspicion I'll be looking for things to do outside of the cabin."

The skin around Graham's eyes crinkled in amusement. "Come over any time."

"I was thinking of outdoorsy stuff." She gestured out the wide windows to the little lake beyond the lodge deck. "I see kayaks. Do you get out much?"

Was that a barely repressed shudder? She elbowed him lightly. "Haven't you been taking advantage of the natural beauty around here?"

Graham's eyes locked on hers for a few seconds, until she nearly forgot her question. "Not much, no."

Was she reading into that gaze? It was like he meant she was the natural beauty. Like he'd truly had a crush on her all those years ago and never quite forgotten it. But that couldn't be. What guy in his twenties liked a girl but never let her know?

Possibly, this one. Which might mean there'd been something off-putting about her, even with an initial spark of attraction. What was wrong with her? Why hadn't he made a move? Was the defect in her the very thing that had attracted Paul? Ugh.

Graham turned away, and the moment was broken. He guided her to the tail end of the lineup and introduced her to the chef, Nadine, and her two assistants.

The middle-aged woman glanced between them as she welcomed Cadence to the ranch. Cadence braced for questions that didn't come. Yet.

Good thing, as she had fewer answers than she'd had even while driving through the night.

They took their trays to a table as the family who'd been sitting there vacated it.

"Let me ask the blessing," Graham said. Without waiting for her response, he bowed his head and offered a quick grace.

Refreshing.

There'd been a lot of things about Paul that she hadn't thought to question. She definitely should have.

Cadence took a bite of her taco salad. "This is really good! If this is a typical meal — and I don't have to cook it myself — this is going to be an amazing summer."

"Roommate notwithstanding?" Graham's eyes twinkled.

"Yeah, even so." She gestured with her fork. "This ranch is the best kept secret ever. And I'm going to make you get out of your shell and take advantage of it. What have you been doing in your free time?"

He stared at her blankly.

"You do have free time, don't you?"

"Not really. We've worked nearly flat-out for the past two-and-a-half months trying to get this place in shape and enticing guests to give us a try."

"You know what they say about Jack?"

"I'm sure you're going to tell me." He forked salad into his mouth.

"All work and no play makes Jack a dull boy." She tapped the back of his hand. "Replace the name Jack with Graham. We wouldn't want a dull Graham."

"Really," he said flatly then took a sip of water.

"Really. So, you're going to play, and if your grandfather thinks you need to be in the office every daylight hour, I'll have a talk with the man."

"Will you now?" Graham gave her a quick glance.

"Sure will. You're the only friend I've got here—"

"Don't forget Paisley."

Cadence rolled her eyes. "How could I? But we're not friends *yet*. So, you're stuck hanging out with me for now. What are the optional activities? Kayaking, horseback riding... what else?"

"Movies. Reading." He pointed his fork at her. "You brought three boxes of books. You must like reading. It's a perfect pastime."

"I've read all those."

"Then why'd you bring them?"

"They're my security blanket, but I'm not going to need them. Not with all this wilderness waiting to be explored."

"Wilderness has its downsides."

"Name one."

"I can name more than one. Mosquitoes. Bears. Rattlesnakes. Mountain lions. Need I go on?"

"Hmm, kayaking sounds better and better, unless that body of water out there harbors sharks."

He chuckled. "You never know."

Oh, she'd made him laugh. Go, her.

IT WAS SUNDAY AFTERNOON, and Graham couldn't believe he was sitting in a flimsy little kayak on a pond. Weren't these things tippy? He didn't mind swimming when he did it on purpose, but he hated surprises. Especially unpleasant ones.

His mind shot back to Wednesday evening and his unplanned dip in Paul's parents' pool. That had been almost like a baptism into a new life. It was the moment his life had changed forever.

He shot a glance to Cadence in the kayak beside him.

She grinned. "Ready?"

"No?"

"You're hilarious."

He hadn't meant to be funny. He meant that he'd rather be reading a thriller on the sofa in his cabin. No mosquitoes buzzed him there. He wasn't too hot or too cold, and there was zero likelihood of an unexpected dunking.

But he hadn't been able to say no to Cadence. Which was something he wasn't about to dissect too deeply. After all, he was responsible for her. Without his intervention, she'd be married to Paul and on her honeymoon somewhere.

"Any regrets?" He couldn't believe the question came out of his mouth.

Cadence's eyebrows drew together beneath her wide-brimmed sun hat. "About the wedding? Only one."

His gut plummeted. "What's that?"

"That I didn't ditch Paul before he ditched me. That I ever thought I saw anything in him worth pursuing."

Graham dared breathe. "Oh."

"You changed my life in all the best ways. Thank you."

She couldn't possibly mean it the way his heart was taking it. "Cool. Now, about this paddle."

"Easy peasy. You dip one end then the other." She pointed hers to an area of lily pads. "Let's head over there."

"Sure." Graham didn't want to let on how incompetent he felt, though she'd probably figured it out. If not, she'd know in the next five minutes. He poked one blade into the water. The small craft was responsive. Maybe he could do this without making a fool of himself.

He kept an eye on the way she paddled and tried to copy her method. She was right. It wasn't rocket science, and the thing wasn't as tippy as it had felt at first. They paddled into the shadows amid large green leaves lying flat on the lake's surface.

"This isn't too terrible." Then a mosquito buzzed his ear, he swatted at it, and the kayak rocked.

Cadence laughed. "I love it. I can practically feel the stress seeping out of me."

Not him. "Maybe that's because of your near escape."

She wrinkled her nose. "At least my mother has

stopped calling a dozen times a day. I mean, I get why she's upset, but you'd think she'd care more about my feelings than about the money. I doubt they remortgaged the house to pay for the wedding or anything crazy like that."

The wedding would have taken place last evening. Graham hadn't taken a full breath until the hour of the ceremony had come and gone. Had he worried she'd fly back to Chicago and marry Paul after all? No. And yet...

"Your church here is nice. Small, but nice."

He blinked at the change of topic. "It's not my church. I'm only here temporarily."

"Why not embrace it while you are?"

"Like you're making me experience this kayak?"

She flashed him a grin. "Next time we're going horse-back riding."

"Did I forget to mention the wildlife?"

"You didn't forget, but I overheard one of the tourists asking Weston about all that at breakfast, and he said sightings were rare and not to worry."

"Easy for him to say."

Cadence dashed her paddle against the surface and sent water arcing toward Graham.

"Oh, girl, do you seriously want to start something?"

She giggled. "I bet you couldn't catch me."

Graham chuckled. He probably couldn't.

"Here." She pulled her phone out of a pocket in her life vest. "Come around behind my kayak, and I'll take a selfie of us to upload to social media."

"Do I have to be in photos?" Yikes, he sounded like a whiny kid.

"You do." She pulled her paddle backward, lining up their watercraft. "Smile. Pretend you're having fun."

He tried, but it would probably look like a grimace. After she'd put the phone away, he said, "we don't even have a social media presence."

"We will by morning. I've been dreaming up a plan."

Of course, she had.

"How's Stephanie's mom doing?"

Graham stared at Cadence for a moment, trying to follow the change in topics. "Have you even met Stephanie?"

"Once. She was in the dining hall with Jamie. He's sure a cutie."

"Yeah, I guess." Tate's charge was barely more than a baby, and his vocabulary was limited to maybe a dozen words and an impressive array of grunts. Maybe someday when the kid was older, Graham could carry on conversations with him.

"Men," Cadence muttered.

"What? Just because I'm not that into other people's kids..."

She pivoted her kayak and stared at him. "You have kids of your own?"

"Of course not." And hopefully she couldn't see the heat that flared up his face.

"Well, I think it's a great thing Tate and Stephanie have done for his nephew, getting married to give him a stable home. I hope they love each other, too."

"I'm sure they do." At least, Tate seemed crazy about his wife.

"It must be hard for them to be apart. Which is why I

asked about Stephanie's mom. They asked for prayer for her in church this morning, remember?"

Yeah, Graham remembered. He was just surprised Cadence had noticed. "Stephanie was supposed to go to Chicago with Tate this week, but then a doctor said her mom might have cancer. They're doing surgery to remove the mass for biopsy this week." See? He'd been paying attention. He cared about what was going on with Tate and his family.

Cadence eyed him. "Gala of the Stars is a big thing for Stephanie to miss now that she's married to Tate. Everyone who's anyone in social circles will attend. Not to mention, word hasn't gone around yet that he's married, so everyone will want to meet Stephanie." She'd gone with Paul last year. This year, they were supposed to be on their honeymoon instead. Narrow escape.

Graham shrugged. "Tate is mostly home to meet up with Justin Chesterman about a merger Sullivan's been working on with Chester Hotels." Not exactly a merger. More like an amicable buyout.

"I hope everything works out okay for them." Cadence pointed her paddle down to the beach by the cottages on Dragonfly Lane. "Let's head over that way."

"Whatever." She might be able to make him get outside, but he didn't have to like it.

CHAPTER SIX

Paisley jogged up to Cadence. "Have you uploaded any photos yet?"

"No, I need to go through them and edit them and see which best represent—"

"Grab your phone and do some candid shots. My kids are putting on a little rodeo over at the corrals."

The Fourth of July was never like this in Chicago. There, Cadence would be dolling up for tonight's gala. Oh… not this year.

"It won't last much longer. Need a lift? I've got one of the golf carts today. Hop on."

Cadence took a quick scan of the grassy area beside the lodge. The sun was angling just right…

Paisley grabbed her arm. "Come on!"

Okay, fine. She clambered aboard. "How long have you been working for Sweet River?"

Paisley zipped down the road toward the stables. "This is my second summer. Working for the Sullivans is way better than with the Smiths last year. They tried. They did, but they simply didn't know how to run a resort like this."

The golf cart veered down a branch in the road, and Cadence caught a glimpse of the signpost. "Pegasus Lane?" she asked in disbelief.

"I know, right? That was the Smiths' idea. All the roads are named for something with wings, like staff housing is on Hummingbird Lane. I don't know why Mr. Sullivan didn't change the names, but he seems amused by them." Paisley hit the brakes beside the corral. "Come on!"

Cadence scrambled off the golf cart and turned her camera on. Paisley might think the shots should be candid and immediate, but that wasn't how she wanted to roll for the most part.

A girl of about ten or eleven ambled a horse around a set of barrels. She wasn't going to win any prizes for speed, but she'd be an easy target for photos.

"Go, Twyla!" Paisley yelled.

The girl smiled, waved, and picked up the pace slightly.

Cadence shot a few photos. More kids followed. She captured them, too. She panned the camera toward the stable doors where a cowboy leaned against the wall with his arms crossed.

As though he heard the click, his glowering gaze fixed on her. Uh oh. No one had told her to avoid any of the staff. She knew she needed parental permission to upload definable photos of kids, but staff?

His frown turned to a cool smirk.

Cadence lowered the camera and stared back, letting her disapproval show. Graham's cousin Weston couldn't scare her. And if the expression he'd morphed to was supposed to be flirting, forget it, buster.

His eyebrows tipped up.

Weston kind of reminded her of Paul right now. So sure of himself that he believed everyone believed the front he put on. That no one could possibly perceive him differently.

"Joke's on you, Weston," she muttered, turning away. "I see right through you."

Paisley elbowed her. "Who're you talking to?"

Oops. "Myself."

"Right." Now it was Paisley doing the disbelieving eyebrow thing.

Cadence turned her back fully on the cowboy and kept her voice low. "That grump is Weston, right? Doesn't he scare the kids away from horseback riding?" Knowing he was in charge of the stables didn't make Cadence want to ride anytime soon.

Paisley rolled her eyes. "It's like he's carrying around his own little storm cloud all the time. Sometimes there's even a little funnel cloud and lightning." She gave a mock shudder. "So terrifying."

Cadence couldn't help chuckling. "I'd ask why they keep him around, but I think I know the answer."

"Nailed it. He's one of the boss's 'new' grandsons, so of course, he won't be canned for being rude to our visitors. He might get demoted, though. Night watchman would be perfect. He'd make any intruders think twice."

The mental picture made Cadence laugh out loud. "He's probably a nice guy under there somewhere."

"I wouldn't bet on it."

"Oh, come on. You're so upbeat. If anyone could make him smile, it would be you."

"You're full of it." Paisley grabbed her arm and pointed. "Did you catch that?"

Cadence whirled back to the corral, but of course, she'd missed whatever had happened. "I'd better focus." She glanced at her roommate again. "Don't give up on the grumpy cowboy so easily."

"I've known him for what, five weeks now? And I haven't seen a genuine smile yet. Not that I'm looking."

"Sure, you are. You optimistically extroverted types can't stand it when everyone isn't like you. It kind of eats at you." Cadence held her breath. That had been a daring thing to say to someone she honestly barely knew.

"Shows what you know. I'm perfectly capable of writing people off if they aren't someone who seems fun to hang around. Life's too short to let a Doogie Downer sprinkle rain on my parade."

"Speaking of parades."

"Right! It's almost time. Get some more shots here and then let's go. The younger kids have been decorating their bikes. And then it's almost time for the chuckwagon. Did you smell that amazing food? They've got ribs in the smoker."

"I did smell it, and I'm already starving."

"And then there's the barn dance and fireworks tonight." Paisley emitted a happy sigh.

"I hear you were the chief planner for all of today's events."

"It's been so much fun! Nadine had the connection with

the chuckwagon people, though, and we were too late to get one of the bigger local bands to perform."

"So, who's doing music?" Not that they were likely a big enough name for Chicago to have heard of them.

"The Delgado brothers from over near Saddle Springs. They're excellent fiddlers, and some of their kids are going to play with them."

Sounded like a boot-stomping, western, good time, and a far cry from the gala taking place soon in Chicago.

Cadence winced. Mom and Dad would likely still go, as would the Bradleys, but whether the two couples would even speak to each other was anyone's guess. She could hope someone else provided a little drama to take the press's mind off the canceled wedding and trying to get statements from their parents.

"Gonna dance tonight?"

Cadence blinked Paisley back into focus. "I... don't know? I've never danced western-style, and I don't know anyone here." Except Graham. Would he ask her? Would she say yes if he did?

One thing was certain. Mr. Grumpy Cowboy over there wouldn't ask. If he did, she'd turn him down. She didn't need that kind of negativity in her life.

GRAHAM STOOD on the lodge steps, feeling out of place in his new clothes even though they were supposed to help him fit in. Grandfather had sent him to Jewel Lake yesterday and told him to buy western duds at From Stetsons to Spurs.

Felicity, the woman who worked there, had been happy to outfit him in jeans, a snap-front shirt, a bandana, a hat, and boots that were actually more comfortable than they looked.

Now Weston could stop griping that he didn't have the proper footwear for riding. Not that Graham wanted to ride. He just didn't want his cousin to make fun of him.

The bandana was over-the-top ridiculous. Graham only spotted a couple of other people wearing one. Maybe he should fold the fabric up and stuff it in his pocket. He loosened the knot.

An elbow poked his ribs as Cadence's floral scent informed him of her presence. "Don't you look all Montanan? Is that what they call people from Montana?"

"I don't know what they're called." He glanced at her and felt his eyes widen. "You cleaned up pretty fine yourself."

She did a little twirl, and her jean skirt flared out around her knees. "Like it? Paisley loaned me this outfit. We're almost the same size." She curtsied.

"You two doing all right together, then?" He hadn't had much chance to talk to her since their kayaking adventure a couple of days ago.

"Yeah. She doesn't talk all the time."

"Just most of the time?"

Cadence laughed. "You've got it right. Seriously, though, she's nice."

"Glad to hear it." Graham could barely take his eyes off Cadence. The cowgirl outfit looked cute on her, different from her usual casual elegance, but still attractive. Then again, he'd think she was beautiful if she were wrapped in a towel. Not that he should think of her dressed in a towel. He ducked his head to hide his flaming cheeks.

"Have you grabbed something to eat yet? Those ribs smell amazing, and there are baked beans and potato salad and a bunch of other kinds of salad, too. Oh, and burgers and sausages and buns. Also, dessert..." Her voice trailed off.

He met her gaze then looked away. If he kept staring at her, drinking her in, she'd know he couldn't keep his thoughts to himself. "I haven't eaten. Why don't we go get in line?"

"Sure. Let's do that." She tucked her hand around his arm, which automatically bent to receive it.

Graham's heart skipped a beat at her casual touch. At her fragrance. At her lilting voice that matched her name. Now he only had to keep his wits about him enough not to trip over air or spill baked beans down this plaid shirt. Not to talk nonsense or recite prime numbers.

One question had been looming over his mind since Friday. Would he have the nerve to ask her to dance? One side of him argued that it was a fun Independence Day celebration, that of course she'd be dancing, probably with a dozen guys. There'd be line dances and square dances and... other kinds. She wouldn't sit on the sidelines. Asking her didn't have to mean anything.

But that's where the opposite side of his brain kicked in. It didn't *have* to mean anything. It likely wouldn't, not to her. But to him? It meant something. It meant he was tongue-tied in her presence and that he'd never gotten over his infatuation of her from way back when.

The trick was not letting on that it mattered to him.

He'd need to play it cool and pretend to be fun. Because, if she was going to dance anyway, he wasn't going to sit back and watch her swinging around with other guys without having a shot at it himself.

She'd be in his arms.

Her fingertips clasped his bicep. There wasn't much to squeeze compared to most of the guys around here. He should start working out.

He hated sweating.

But he didn't want Cadence to think he was just another wimpy city boy.

"DANCE WITH ME?" Cadence held her hand out to Graham as she rose to her feet. The Delgado duo had struck up a lively tune.

"I…" He looked startled. "Sure."

"Too forward?" She angled her head as he stood and wiped his palms down those stiff dark blue jeans.

"No. I was going to ask you anyway, but I was getting my nerve together."

"Nerve?" She angled her head at him as she took his hand. "It's too beautiful a night not to dance, and you're the only person here I know at all."

He looked away.

Cadence replayed the words inside her head. "I'm sorry. That made it sound like you would have been my last choice, which is totally not true. Still, it's a fact I don't know anyone else."

Graham set his hand on her waist and offered a

guarded smile. "That's fair enough. And I probably know you better than I know anyone else here."

She looked up at him as they began to step to the music. "But you've been here for three months. And we didn't know each other all that well in college."

He swallowed hard. "I noticed you, though."

"You did? You never let on."

"I'm not good at this. Not good at talking about anything but numbers or maybe books."

"Yet you called out Paul on marrying me when he said he didn't love me."

His eyes locked on hers. "What did you hear?"

Cadence shrugged. "One of my bridesmaids is dating one of the groomsmen. He told her what went down. You stuck out your neck for me."

"And took a dunking for it." He managed a chuckle.

"So, I think you're my hero, and that's why I wanted this dance."

"And maybe another one?"

She squeezed their clasped hands. "You might be able to talk me into a dozen."

Graham's fingers lightly pressed against her waist. "I'd like to think I'd have stuck my oar into Paul's monologue even if it hadn't been you, but I'm not sure I would have. All I knew for sure was that you deserved better treatment than that."

"Thank you."

"I'm… I know you've got stuff to think about after what happened. I get that. And I also know that a beautiful, accomplished woman like you will have all kinds of guys lined up in no time at all. So, thanks for tonight."

He didn't think he was the kind of man she'd go for? All he had to go by was public evidence. She'd settled for Paul Bradley.

But he was also right. It had only been a week since she'd been dumped. She needed time to process it all.

She twirled, and he dipped her. Their gazes met for a long moment before he righted her. They stepped back into the flow on the makeshift dance floor.

"Why don't we see where things lead us?" she suggested. *God.* She meant where God led them. One of the places He was leading her was into remembering she trusted Him. She'd been so busy — no, self-absorbed — the last while, she'd been negligent.

Graham's smile was fleeting. "Sounds fair."

A few minutes later, Bryce cut in, and Graham stepped aside. The next time she looked for him, he'd disappeared.

CHAPTER SEVEN

C adence's eyes took a moment to adjust to the dim interior of the stable. Ahh. A smile crept across her face as the tension oozed away. Stalls for more than a dozen horses lined the concrete center aisle, which was spotlessly clean. The scent of fresh straw filled her nostrils, and the gentle sound of a tail swishing against planks met her ears. Further out, she could hear voices and laughter.

This took her way back to her childhood summers at camp in the best possible of ways. The little girl she'd been had lived for those weeks hanging out with her equally horse-crazy friends and the equines they all adored. She'd kept going as a helper even as a teen, when many of her friends had been flaunting their trips abroad.

She'd been here for a full two weeks, and this was her first visit to the stables with intent to ride. The first time she'd been able to convince Graham.

Why did it matter if he came along? Cadence didn't want to think about it. She was the one who loved to ride.

He proclaimed hating it. She could have ridden without him anytime.

A shadow crossed the brightly lit doorway at the other end. When the person stepped beyond the illumination, she could see it was Weston. Maybe that's why she hadn't come. He wasn't her favorite person, and she wasn't as kind and forgiving as her housemate. Paisley had decided the grouchy cowboy was going to learn to smile. *Good luck with that, girl.*

"I thought you said Graham was coming."

"He'll be here in a minute."

Weston rolled his eyes. "Maybe I'll wait to saddle Kennedy when he actually shows up."

Cadence's back stiffened. "He's coming. He said so."

"Sure. Whatever. I thought I'd put you on Mirage." Weston crossed to a box stall and opened it. "Hey, girl. Wanna go for a trail ride?"

Cadence blinked. The guy's whole voice and demeanor changed when he spoke with a horse. She edged closer to see him running his hands through the palomino's mane and cupping her head.

"She's beautiful."

Weston's hands dropped as he turned to her. "Yeah, she is. You say you've done a lot of riding?"

"A fair bit." Her gaze landed on the saddle on its block. "I can tack up."

His eyed her skeptically before he stepped back and crossed his arms. "I'll watch."

Or he could do whatever else he needed to do. But she got it. Probably dozens of people told him they'd ridden lots when they hadn't.

Cadence entered the stall and introduced herself to Mirage before beginning the process. She was adjusting the cinch when she heard footsteps in the aisle.

"You came." Weston's voice was noncommittal.

"I said I would," Graham replied.

"I thought you'd back out."

"Why would you think that about me?"

Cadence glanced over. Both guys glared at each other. No love lost. What would it take for them to actually become friends? She needed to think on that. Not that she wanted to hang out with Weston, exactly, but it wasn't his fault he hadn't known this side of his family until recently. Feeling defensive seemed reasonable under the circumstances.

"You rode Kennedy last time. Okay with the same choice today?"

"Sure."

Weston pivoted on his booted heel and entered the box stall across from Mirage's, Graham trailing behind.

"I'll saddle up for you. Your girlfriend there did a good job on hers, but you don't have the experience."

Girlfriend? Cadence stiffened.

"She's not my girlfriend."

Had she expected him to claim that status? Of course not. He'd rescued her. That was all. There might be something in his eyes at times — like at the barn dance — but he didn't feel strongly enough about her to make a move. He hadn't in college, and he didn't now.

Did she want him to?

Cadence turned away from the men and wrapped her arms around Mirage's neck.

No, she didn't. She should still be getting over Paul Bradley. Because she should have loved him passionately.

She wasn't. She hadn't. She'd had no business marrying him. Thankfully, he'd broken things off at the last minute or she'd just now be returning from her honeymoon with a man she was barely in mutual tolerance with. What a close call.

Maybe her feelings for Graham were simply because he'd rescued her. Wasn't there some sort of mental disorder like that? She was attracted to him because he'd saved her.

Also, maybe a bit because he was unerringly kind and polite and unassuming. Because he seemed to need someone to actually see him as the great guy he didn't think he was.

His Sullivan cousins were nice enough. Tate was back from his week in Chicago and, though there'd been some drama surrounding the Gala of the Stars, he and Stephanie looked like they'd worked through it. Bryce was okay. He seemed a little too full of himself for Cadence's taste. Since he hadn't directed that attitude at her, she could ignore him. Maxwell was focused on the renovations on the cabins and didn't even show up for meals half the time.

Weston and Jude seemed opposite each other. Weston had a chip on his shoulder, while Jude seemed quiet and unassuming. More like Graham in some ways.

Huh.

Graham's voice came from behind her. "Ready?"

Cadence turned a bright smile in his direction. "So ready."

"You're sure you don't need me along?" Weston looked between them.

"We'll be fine." Cadence led Mirage out past the guys and through the open doorway before swinging into the saddle. Ah, she'd missed this in the past few years. She glanced back to see Graham struggling to mount, but he made it up, so kudos to him.

She looked over at Weston. "We'll be going up the south trail. The map says that's about a two-hour ride?"

"About that. I'll give you three before I come looking for you." The surly cowboy smirked. "In case you meet a grizzly or something."

They weren't going to need rescuing, but Cadence bit her tongue and nodded. She squeezed her knees into Mirage's flanks. "Let's go, girl."

Graham nudged Kennedy up beside her as soon as the trail was wide enough.

She glanced over. "You doing okay?" Because he looked ramrod stiff.

"Sure."

"Relax a little and go with the flow."

He shot her a glare. "I'm relaxed."

"Whatever you say." She chuckled. "Thank you for agreeing to come with me today." Maybe she should have taken Paisley up on the offer to ride with the group of teens she'd be taking out this afternoon instead of pushing Graham. Fact was, she preferred Graham's company.

That was the transference syndrome or whatever it was called rearing its head again. It was too soon after Paul to actually fall for someone else. And Graham wasn't the kind of guy she'd normally go for, so the interest she felt couldn't be real.

She'd keep telling herself that.

AND SHE TOLD him to relax.

How on earth could he stay in the saddle if he relaxed? He'd probably slide right off like a sack of potatoes if he didn't focus on his balance and keep his heels down and his reins positioned properly.

And then there was Weston's dig about bears. *Thanks a lot.*

But it was a lovely morning. Cadence had been right about that. The sun angled through the aspens at this elevation. A rainstorm had come through last night, and the air smelled fresh.

Not as sweet as Cadence smelled, not that he was about to mention it. Sitting on a horse kept him from leaning in a little to sniff her floral fragrance. He'd noticed her aromatic preferences on the road trip west and been hyper aware of it since the dance a couple of weeks ago.

Today she'd smell like horse.

That wouldn't be a turn-off, actually. There was little he could imagine about her that would do that to him.

And he needed to rein in those thoughts. He'd been trying to do that for the past few weeks, but with little success so far.

Cadence breezed through the office several times a day, distracting him from the spreadsheets and workbooks that filled his screen and usually kept him well occupied. She had a small desk angled into a corner of the office, a nook she'd made her own with photos of the ranch sticky-tacked to the wall. He was in a couple of them, but he wasn't going to read too much into that, since many of the shots had other people in them.

Graham managed to lift his gaze from the trail directly between his horse's ears and take a deeper breath. Maybe he could adjust his body to the rhythm. He well remembered how stiff he'd been last time after fighting it the entire ride. But how did one even do that?

He glanced at Cadence.

She beamed back at him. "Isn't this fun?"

Fun. He wouldn't put it that way. But with her? "Sure."

"You're lying." She giggled, the sound like tinkling bells.

Man, he was a goner. He should never have invited her to Montana when he knew her presence would only fan the flame he'd managed to douse years ago. But he couldn't have left her there to pick up all the pieces when he had solutions for every single one of her challenges. The result? He had the privilege — he snorted quietly — of ignoring the attraction that had flared to life since that evening in Chicago.

"What are you thinking?" Her quiet question seemed genuine.

"Uh…" He couldn't let on what he thought of her. What if she regretted everything? But it didn't seem like it. "Heard anything from Paul?"

"I blocked his number weeks ago."

"He doesn't have your email?"

She sighed. "Yeah, he does. He's emailed a bunch of times, so I finally set a filter to send them straight to trash."

"You haven't even read them?" Graham shouldn't allow his hopes to dance. "He might be genuinely sorry."

"It's too late. Much, much too late." Cadence offered him a wry grin. "That was a super close call. Thanks again for the rescue."

"Anyone would have helped."

"I doubt it. He had nine other groomsmen, but only one called him out. I owe you everything."

She didn't mean it the way his stupid heart wanted to take it.

"Uh, how are your parents doing? Is your mom still guilting you?"

Cadence wrinkled her nose. "They plan to come visit, but I'm not sure I want them to. I'm liable to get an earful, and everyone in the vicinity will find out what an ungrateful wretch I am."

Graham studied her expression as the horses ambled out into an open meadow. "Did they so badly want you to marry someone you didn't love that they wouldn't understand?"

"It's the money and the embarrassment. My mother says I could have handled things better. And she might be right."

"How so?"

"Well, I didn't want to face the fact that our relationship wasn't based on love and mutual respect. I could have — should have — owned up to that months ago and broken up with Paul. Long before the invoices started rolling in."

Graham mulled her answer. "Why didn't you?"

"The million-dollar question, for sure. I guess I naively thought things would get better? That we'd be okay?

Mostly, I tried not to think about it." She let out a long breath. "I was a coward."

Graham chuckled. "And here I thought that word was reserved for me. I've never been one to stick out my neck for what I wanted. It's easier to go with the flow and hope for the best."

"You?" Cadence shifted in her saddle to search his face. "You were plenty brave to call Paul out."

He gulped. "Something came over me."

"Like what?"

Man, he didn't want to go here. "I can't bear when people are mistreated."

"That's noble, but people are mistreated all the time."

"Because it was *you*, okay?" Heat infused his face, and he was pretty sure it wasn't the sunshine.

"I used to wonder, back in college, if you had a thing for me."

Right now would be the perfect time for a rockslide or a flash of lighting or even a mountain lion sighting. But no. He cleared his throat. "Kind of."

"Why didn't you say anything?"

Seriously? He glanced at her, but he couldn't sustain eye contact. Not when it was this personal. He wasn't ready to pin his heart on his sleeve. Didn't know if he ever would be. "I wasn't the type of guy a girl like you would notice."

"I noticed you."

"I mean, *that* way. You dated the jocks in college. You were in the middle of the in crowd. I... was neither."

"Guys like you weren't interested in girls like me. Just the fact that you never made a move proved that to me."

Come again? Graham scratched his neck. She didn't

make any sense. He remembered their college years. He'd been bookish and withdrawn. He'd lived for chess club, because it was a safe place. A place where he hung out among equals. Was respected. Didn't have to prove anything.

He couldn't be hearing her correctly. Why would she have been in the popular group if she didn't belong there? Of course, she belonged. She was pretty. Vivacious. As sweet as she looked.

Some guy a whole lot better than Paul should have seen the treasure she was long ago.

Someone a whole lot better than Graham. Someone different. Someone like... Maxwell, maybe. Nice guy. Hard worker. Respectful. Though he might be a little young for Cadence...

But why not Graham? Didn't they already have a wee bit of a connection? He'd admitted it. She'd admitted noticing him. And he had a clear playing field here at Sweet River Ranch. No competition in the running that he could tell.

Wasn't she still mourning a broken relationship?

It didn't sound like it. Maybe... maybe he should stop being a chicken.

He looked over at her, this time holding contact for more than a fleeting second. "Are you telling me we were both aware of each other back then, and neither of us did anything about it?"

She lifted a shoulder and offered a wry grin. "Sounds like it. I guess I was waiting for the guy to make the first move the way my parents taught me."

"And the other guys did."

"Yeah."

Graham shook his head. How did a man embrace bravery, especially in relationships? "My loss."

She tipped up her eyebrows.

Man, she was gorgeous. He sucked in a deep breath. "But, hey, we're both here now."

A smile twitched at her lips.

"So... this is me, thinking about making a move. Years after the fact." What a dorky thing to say.

"This is me, observing your move. Seeing *you*."

Now what was he supposed to do? Climb off his horse and kiss her? He might never make it back in Kennedy's saddle. Besides, they weren't at the kissing stage. They were barely at the acknowledging stage.

Graham cleared his throat. Wow, there was a lot of phlegm in there choking him off. "So... this is us."

She grinned.

"And your parents are coming when?"

Her smile dimmed. "Next week, I think."

Was he going to let them know what he thought of their daughter? Ugh. Time would tell.

CHAPTER EIGHT

Paisley glanced up as Cadence came in the door, and her eyes narrowed. "What happened on your ride?"

Cadence tried to wipe the smile off her face. Failed. "Why? What do you mean?"

"You look like the cat who caught the canary."

"Yuck. Who wants to snare a scrawny bird?"

"The diversion isn't working."

Couldn't blame a girl for trying. Cadence focused on toeing off her cowboy boots. Was she actually ready to let anyone know that she and Graham had sort of acknowledged a mutual attraction?

"Did he kiss you?"

Startled, Cadence whirled around. "What?"

"Graham. Did he kiss you?"

"At least you didn't mean Weston."

Paisley wrinkled her nose. "Nice try. To the best of my knowledge, you haven't spent the past few weeks pretending you didn't have a thing for Mr. Grumpy Cowboy."

"Because I don't?"

"Exactly!" Paisley offered three slow claps. "Now spill. I need the details."

"There's nothing to tell."

"Why are you making this so difficult?"

"Why do you care so much?"

"Someone around here needs to make a move. I've seen how the two of you pretend not to be aware of each other, sneaking peeks when you think the other one won't notice."

Cadence had noticed, all right. "Do I need to remind you that a month ago, I expected to marry someone else in just a few days?"

"Your point?"

Did she need to spell everything out? "Because how can I trust myself now? I made a huge mistake, and God offered me an exit ramp at the last instant. I'm so thankful for that, but I would have followed through if Paul hadn't badmouthed me at his bachelor party. If Graham hadn't stood up for me."

"But that didn't happen. You got a reprieve. Do you feel like you're on the rebound?"

Cadence winced. "Wouldn't I have had to be in love with Paul to be on the rebound now? I mean, I should have been in love with him to marry him…" Her thoughts drifted off and took her words with them.

"So, you didn't love Paul, and you're not on the rebound."

"I'm not sure. I mean, I know I didn't love Paul. Not the

way I should have to marry him. But maybe the problem is me. Maybe I don't know how to love."

Paisley surged to her feet, crossed the space, and gripped Cadence's shoulders. "I don't believe that for one red hot second. Have you forgotten what Paul said about using you? You told me what Graham told you."

Cadence looked at the floor. "Maybe I read into it."

"Do you believe that?"

She let out a shaky breath. "No? But I must be a bad person if the person who should have cherished me above all others was only using me." Man, it was hard getting that out. Admitting it.

"He wasn't the person who should have cherished you above all others."

"What do you mean?" Cadence met Paisley's eyes. "He was my fiancé!"

"I know, but you're well rid of him. Granted, I never met the guy and hope I never do, because I'd give him a piece of my mind. But you... you're a great person. Is it terrible I'm glad they ran out of staff housing and needed to double up? That Mr. Sullivan put us together? I'm super thankful."

Tears prickled at Cadence's eyes. "Thanks. I appreciate you, too." She enfolded her housemate in a hug.

A moment later, Paisley stepped back. "So, back to the trail ride. Graham didn't kiss you. Did you wish he would?"

"No." Liar.

"Do you like him?"

"Of course, I do. What's not to like?"

"Right, since he rescued you from a nasty situation. But you'd known him aside from Paul?"

"We were all in college together."

Paisley shook her head. "Wait. You had a crush on him back then?"

"I knew who he was, that's all. He seemed to maybe like me, but he never said anything. Never did anything."

"He comes across as rather shy."

Cadence let out a breath. "I didn't see that then. He was a brainiac, and I really wasn't. And I didn't hang out with them, either. They weren't cool enough for College Girl Cadence. I got my schoolwork done, but I was there for the parties. The social connections."

"That was then, and this is now."

"Yeah." Cadence sighed. "I wish I'd given Graham an opportunity back then. Even just been nice to him."

"Most kids that age are only thinking of themselves. You're hardly alone in that."

"Said from the wise old age of...?" Cadence tilted her head at her housemate.

"Eight years later." Paisley laughed. "But it's still true, isn't it?"

"It is. Sadly."

"What are you going to do about Graham now? Give him a chance?"

"Maybe?"

Paisley squealed.

"But I'm honestly not sure it's a good idea."

"Whyever not?"

"I feel like such a flake. Engaged to one guy and didn't even have the nerve to break it off myself. And now, a mere few weeks later, thinking I can be in a healthy relationship with someone else? Doesn't that seem — I don't know — wrong?"

"No one's going to judge you for that, girl."

"I judge myself."

"No one *else* is going to."

Cadence strode into the kitchen then pivoted and crossed her arms over her chest. "How can they not? My parents are still experiencing the fall-out of the canceled wedding. Did I tell you they're coming next week? I'm going to hear all about it, over and over and *over* again. If I'm under any illusions about moving on, they'll make sure I remember that I'm still shackled."

Paisley studied her. "There's a lot to unpack in there."

"Tell me," Cadence muttered.

"They're staying at the lodge?"

"But of course. The cottages would be far too rustic for the likes of Daniel and Amelia Foster. Cook for themselves in a rental? Ha!"

"I see." Paisley slumped onto the sofa. "Are they going to talk you into going back home?"

"They're going to try, but they won't succeed. My father is looking for a job for me worthy of a Foster. My mother thinks I need to move back in with them so I can heal."

Paisley grimaced.

"Exactly. I promised Mr. Sullivan through Labor Day, but as my mother pointed out, I also promised to marry Paul, so my word isn't particularly reliable."

"Ouch. What does Graham think of all that?"

"He knows my parents are coming. I don't know that he's exactly prepared for their onslaught, though. My mother especially is such a bulldozer."

"You're lucky."

Cadence blinked. "Come again?"

"My mother barely remembers I exist between one drug high and the next."

"I'm so sorry." Cadence dropped onto the sofa beside her friend and wrapped an arm around her. "I can't even imagine."

"What's going on?" Tate leaned back in his office chair and studied Graham.

"Me? Nothing."

"Obviously something."

Graham shot a glance at his cousin. "Did I screw up the payroll? I went through it three times."

Tate shook his head. "Although you do seem distracted."

"There's a lot of pressure, what with all the parental units coming to analyze the ranch next week."

Tate grimaced. "That is true. My father is grouching because Grandfather is sending him to Kansas to pick up my mother again. He says someone else needs to get their pilot's license. Either that, or Grandfather needs to revert to having all the board meetings in Chicago, so Mom can fly commercial from Wichita."

At least the conversation had been diverted. "Count me off the potential pilot list. My vision isn't good enough." Which was fine with Graham. The thought of being in control of a flying object and the passengers within was terrifying. Had been terrifying even before Wally's helicopter had crashed and killed all four onboard.

"I almost wish I had that excuse. Truth is, Wally is the only one of us who ever wanted to fly." Tate tipped a pen end over end. "Jude said something the other day about it, though. He might want to take up the mantle, as it were."

"Jude?" Graham tried to keep the shock out of his voice. Failed.

"Our cousin Jude." Tate chuckled. "Grandfather will give him the opportunity if he wants it. They're looking into the requirements."

Graham scratched his neck. How had he managed not to know this was coming? Had he been that focused on Cadence he'd been oblivious to all else? Possibly.

Also, he'd been thinking about her parents' visit to Sweet River without putting two and two together and realizing his own parents would be here on business at the same time. Ugh. This was not going to be pleasant.

"Cadence seems to be doing good work."

Graham refocused on his cousin. "The website looks a lot better, right? No offense to your mother."

"Mom knows more than most of the rest of us about the basics of site creation, but it's not her passion. She's happy Cadence has been able to build on the platform she put in place. It looks inviting now."

"She takes great photos, too."

"You seem to be in a lot of them."

Graham's gaze swung to meet his cousin's as though he couldn't control it.

Tate smirked. "Anything going on that we should know about?"

"Just because you're married now doesn't mean everyone else is busy falling in love or anything like that."

Tate raised his eyebrows. "That was very specific."

A burn crept up Graham's cheeks. "She's nice. I like her. I also like Paisley, and I like Heather, and I like Kaci."

"Starting a harem?" Tate chuckled.

"You're hilarious."

"I thought so." He leaned onto his desk and studied Graham. "Do you like her a little more than the others?"

Graham thought back to their horseback ride a few days ago. He'd had such a good time with her he'd nearly forgotten he'd been high up on a potentially deadly beast. They'd talked, gotten to know each other better, and admitted they each might have feelings. Preliminary ones, but feelings all the same. He glanced back at his cousin. "Maybe."

"Good for you."

He blinked. "Really?"

"Sure, why not? She complements you in many ways. She gets you out of your shell…"

"I have a shell?"

Tate laughed. "Isn't that what you call it when a person hunkers away from everyone else as soon as office hours are over?"

"The doors are never locked around here." Graham sighed. "At least, they weren't before you put your foot down with Grandfather. I'm not sure I ever thanked you properly for that."

It had been a few weeks since Tate's return from Chicago. Their grandsire had confirmed Tate as the main decision maker for Sweet River Ranch. Graham could only be grateful it wasn't him… as well as grateful that Tate had refused to allow more than one evening meeting per week going forward. Plus, he'd insisted on actual weekends off.

"That pace wasn't sustainable." Tate studied Graham. "I'm not sure why our grandmother put up with it, but it wrecked my parents' marriage, and Wally and Ashley weren't doing so great, either."

"I think my parents only handle it because they each do their own thing most of the time, anyway. It suits them to remain together and show a united front."

"A power couple."

Graham sighed. "Something like that. I have to say, I admire your mom for making a stand. She still manages to work for Sullivan and have an actual life of her own. Has she been seeing anyone?"

Tate shook his head. "Not that I know of. I spent months with her in Gilead over the winter, so I'm pretty sure I'd know."

"It's complicated being a Sullivan."

"Tell me."

Were Graham and his cousin actually becoming friends through this project of Grandfather's? Maybe it was a good thing.

Graham was going to miss Tate when he began working out of the Chicago office again. Maybe Tate had the right idea — he and Stephanie were drawing up plans to build a house on the ranch. Graham could, too.

Mountain lions. Grizzly bears. Rattlesnakes. He hadn't seen a single one of any of those creatures, and he'd die happy if he never did. Chicago was blessedly free of any and all.

Humans committing crimes against humans, on the

other hand, was a much greater problem back home than here. As were noise and pollution.

But there were so many good things about urban life. He'd spent his entire life — until April of this year — living within city limits. It was home in a way his side of a staff duplex never could be.

Tate was putting down roots here. Making a home for Stephanie and Jamie.

That wasn't for Graham. He had no desire to be a rancher or even a ruralist. Peace and quiet were nice, though. Books and movies could be his companions anywhere he hung his hat.

What about Cadence? Did she miss the city? Would she scurry back to Chicago in September and leave Sweet River Ranch behind without a backward glance? She probably would.

She'd leave him behind even if he returned to Chicago himself, which he would, of course. Someone like her wouldn't be satisfied with a guy like him for the long-term. She didn't have as many options here, plus there was the whole rescue thing.

He'd lose her to the fast-paced life, sooner or later.

She might not see it yet, but she would. He needed to be watchful.

CHAPTER NINE

> We've landed in this godforsaken airport with another hour to get to this ranch on the backside of beyond. And I don't even want to talk about what they consider a suitable rental car in Montana.

C adence bit her lip at her mother's text. It wasn't like she'd invited her parents to visit Sweet River. Although, she should have. She should be grateful they cared enough to check up on her. She'd treated them abominably.

No, Paul Bradley had treated them all that way. It hadn't been her. All she'd done was accept his rejection and leave town. Possibly driving for two days might seem excessive to her parents, but that's where the refuge Graham offered had been. If it had been in a different direction, a different distance, that's where she would have gone.

But... Graham Sullivan.

What an enigma. They'd had a moment last week on

the trail ride where they'd both seemed to acknowledge feelings. At least, that's what she'd done, and what she thought he'd said in return at the time.

But they'd gone back to awkward and possibly to avoidance, if Graham's increased absence from the office was any indication. He always seemed to be busy... or elsewhere.

Had she misheard his words? No, he'd clearly said he was making a move. Possibly the guy played chess and contemplated upcoming moves for hours or days at a time.

Possibly he'd changed his mind. Should she ask? Because it would be nice to know exactly where she stood with Graham before her parents arrived. She'd been so hopeful...

To ask him, she'd have to find him.

Then that's exactly what she'd do. Cadence pushed back from her desk.

Tate glanced up from his workspace nearer the door.

She took a deep breath. "Do you have any idea where Graham is? I need to talk to him."

Tate studied her.

So, he did know something. She tilted her eyebrows up.

"He had a meeting with Maxwell's team an hour ago over in the conference room, reevaluating budgets."

"Think the meeting is still ongoing?"

"Could be. Not sure."

It was something to go on, anyway. "Thanks." She strode out of the office, down the corridor, across the great room, and into the other wing.

The conference room doors opened at her arrival, and

Maxwell, Heather, and several of their team exited, chatting among themselves.

Cadence ducked into the room as the last of them left. There he was. Her heart sped up.

Graham stood by the wall screen, flipped his laptop closed, and glanced up.

"Hi, Graham."

"Hi." His gaze seemed to measure the distance to the exit before coming back to her.

Which basically told her at least part of what she needed to know. He'd definitely been avoiding her. Cadence wrapped her arms around her midsection and studied him. "I've missed seeing you." It was kind of surprising how much.

"Yeah. About that…" He adjusted his glasses.

They weren't even really together, and he was going to dump her? After extracting a promise to stay for ten weeks? They weren't even halfway through.

"What, Graham? Did you change your mind? Did you realize you only like rescuing damsels in distress but don't actually want a relationship?"

"That's not it."

"Then what?" What had come over her? She wasn't normally this forward. But maybe she'd never had a taste of something worth fighting for before. "My parents will be here shortly, and I need to know where we stand. I thought you'd said you wanted to explore something with me."

His gaze slid past her face. "You're on the rebound. I forgot that. I mis-stepped."

"Pfft."

That got his attention.

Cadence took a few steps closer, holding his gaze. "I thought we'd covered that already. Paul was a mistake. I didn't love him, and he didn't love me. Marrying him would have been the stupidest thing I've ever done, and that's saying something. I'm not mourning the loss of a great romance. I'm far too busy kicking myself in the rear for being blind and stupid."

She was probably making another mistake right now. Graham didn't love her any more than his cousin had. Why should he? She'd been as flighty as a summer breeze. Now from the east, now from the south. Now here, now gone.

No more.

Graham shifted from one foot to the other. "It's too soon for you to know that. I shouldn't have pushed you."

For the love. "You didn't push me. And it is not too soon." Cadence closed the gap, grabbed Graham by the front of his shirt, stood on tiptoes, and kissed him.

His lips were unyielding against hers for several long seconds before softening. Then his arms came around her, and he took control of the kiss.

Cadence savored his lips, the taste of him. He'd said he hadn't dated much, but his mouth definitely knew how to do this kissing thing. She clenched his shirt tighter with one hand and cupped the other around the back of his neck, holding him in place lest he get any ideas about cutting this moment short.

A gasp came from behind her. Great, some guest or employee had caught an eyeful. Whatever.

A low, deep chuckle followed the gasp.

Cadence froze. She knew that sound. She dropped to

her heels, breaking the kiss. Graham immediately released her, and she chilled where his hands had been as she slowly turned to face the door.

Mom. Dad.

And Paul Bradley. What in heaven's name was her ex doing at Sweet River Ranch? His eyebrows were tipped up to match the sardonic grin on the lower part of his face, but his eyes…

Cadence chilled.

Paul's icy blue eyes said someone was going to pay.

Mom's wide gaze darted between Cadence, Graham, and Paul, but her hand covered her mouth.

Dad shook his head, turned on his heel, and stalked out, the clip of his dress shoes sounding on the plank floors. Didn't that figure?

"Cadence Marie Foster! How could you?"

How was it Mom managed to sound like the one aggrieved?

Cadence tipped her chin up. "How could I what?"

"I knew something suspicious was up when he came to the house that night. Dripping wet."

"Dripping wet because Paul threw him in the pool."

"I didn't touch him." Paul shook his head as he raised both hands defensively. "I never would. Not my cousin Gray."

"Okay, so your henchmen did."

"Henchmen?" Paul smirked. "You mean my very good friends. All but one had my best interests at heart." His gaze hardened on Graham.

Cadence stared at the man she'd once thought she loved. "Did Graham make up the story? That you wished you didn't have to marry me... and then realized you didn't have to, since the business contacts had already been shared? Did you tell him to tell me and to get your ring back?"

"Aw, babe. It wasn't that way."

Behind her, Graham shifted, but she didn't dare glance at him to see how he was taking the rebuttal.

"I'd had a little much to drink. You know how pushy Darrell can be. Booze loosened my tongue, and I regret it."

"Booze doesn't usually make up things that don't exist."

Paul spread his hands. "I'm sorry?"

Sure, he was.

"You should listen to Paul. He's sorry, honey. Didn't you hear him? Everything can be salvaged. We've lost some deposits, sure, but others will still be valid if we rebook soon—"

"No."

"Babe." Paul took a few steps toward her.

Those eyes. Why had she never seen the icy glitter in those blue orbs before? "Don't you dare come any closer. I'm not your babe, and this conversation is over."

"Now, Cadence," Mom began.

"Mother. I thought you and Dad were coming to visit me. To see where I've landed up, meet my new friends—"

"Graham Sullivan isn't a new friend, and it seems he's taken a lot of liberty with a woman engaged to someone else."

Cadence blew out an exasperated breath. "I'm not engaged to anyone. Paul broke it off, and I returned the ring. I'm free to make my own choices."

"Not so free." Paul shuddered dramatically. "Your father has made some stipulations."

The father who had disappeared out of the conference room the instant the pressure increased? How dare he suggest any terms?

"It seems your father held back some key information in the merger deals. So, yes, we're getting married."

"We are so not getting married."

"Honey, you need to think this through," Mom implored. "Not only did your father hold back, but so did Donald Bradley."

"This is my problem how?"

Dad's voice came from the doorway. "It becomes your problem when your inheritance gets cut off."

A PIN COULD HAVE DROPPED and sounded like an explosion in the aftermath of Daniel Foster's threat.

Graham had plummeted from the highest high in his life to the lowest low in the space of mere seconds, even lower than when he'd heard of Cadence and Paul's engagement.

He'd been a fool to let a week go by without staking his claim, but he'd been certain she'd regretted it. He'd been a fool to get his hopes up in the first place. He'd *known* she was on the rebound, no matter what she said. He should have protected her heart, should have encouraged her to forgive Paul.

Should he really?

Not by the harsh gleam in his cousin's eye. Paul needed

Cadence to fulfill the business arrangement. Cadence needed Paul to keep her inheritance, because Daniel Foster didn't look like he was bluffing.

But… she didn't need anything from her parents if she married Graham. He could wipe aside her problems with little effort. He took a step backward as the thought slammed into his chest.

No, he couldn't add to the insanity in front of him by suggesting that. They'd acknowledged basic feelings last week. Perhaps acknowledged some passion in the kiss they'd shared moments ago. Neither was enough to base a marriage on.

Neither were threats nor the punitive expression Paul wore, but Graham didn't have the right to interfere. This was something Cadence needed to decide. All he could do was pray.

"You promised, honey," her mother begged. "We'll forgive you. Please come home, and let's give this another try."

Cadence shook her head and backed up. "No. I'm not bound by last year's poor decision. I'm not returning to Chicago, and I'm not marrying Paul. Cut me off if you must."

Graham's heart swelled at her bravery in calling their bluff. *Thank You, Lord. Help her stick to it.*

Paul smirked and beckoned Daniel Foster closer, gesturing him to speak as though introducing a grand master to the stage.

"It's not as simple as all that, Cadence," Daniel began. "This debacle can ruin us. If we cut you off, it's only because we'll be penniless ourselves."

Say what? The situation couldn't be that dire, could it? A glance at Paul's sneering face, and Graham wasn't so sure.

Amelia Foster choked back sobs and turned away, covering her face.

Cadence crossed to her mother and reached for her, but Amelia flinched away. Cadence turned slowly back to the room, her arms tight around her waist.

The five of them in the room seemed at an impasse, each waiting for someone else to break the tension.

Paul eyed Graham and thumbed toward the exit. The message was clear. Graham was being dismissed as inconsequential.

Cadence had come to him only minutes ago. Had kissed him fervently. Did that count for anything? Should he stand by her now, or should he let her make her own decisions?

It seemed she had enough people telling her what to do, though, granted, the others all wanted the same thing: for her to capitulate. So, was Graham supposed to pull her the other direction?

He couldn't do it.

But he also couldn't abandon her to the wolves. "Cadence?"

Her gaze flew to meet his. "Yes?"

"I'm needed back in the office. Please come find me when you're ready." Ready for what? Graham couldn't have said. Then he nodded stiffly at Cadence's father. "I assume you've checked in? Dinner will be served in the dining room shortly. We have an excellent chef. I'm sure you won't be disappointed."

Graham kept his cool and nodded at Paul, managing

not to walk over and slug the guy. He knew how that would go down. Paul had muscles where Graham had nothing. Being tossed into the pool would seem like mercy compared to being punched.

He measured his strides to the door and down the corridor and didn't dare breathe until he entered the great room. Then he sagged into the nearest leather chair, took off his glasses, and rubbed his face in his hands.

Had he done the right thing?

How was a guy supposed to know? No one was going to hurt Cadence, not in the lodge. They weren't going to kidnap her and force her to return to Chicago. Was he absolutely certain of that? Fairly. At least in the short term. They were still trying to appeal to Cadence's sense of family loyalty.

Her parents didn't deserve her allegiance. Not if they were using her the way it sounded like. None of them loved Cadence the way she deserved. Not her parents. For sure not Paul.

But what did Graham know of love? His parents remained together simply because it was too much hassle and expense to separate. They knew they were stronger together, and the value of that unified front overrode everything else.

Look at Uncle James and Aunt Maribel. They'd divorced years ago because Sullivan Enterprises drove a wedge between them. But it also kept them together, because neither had given up their positions within the family company.

Money — and the love of it — did that to people. It

drove Uncle Donald and Aunt Frances. It definitely drove their son, Paul. It was driving the Fosters.

Did it drive Graham?

He wouldn't have thought so, but now he wondered.

Who would he be without the Sullivan money? Without the Sullivan name? Without the Sullivan position?

Graham would be an average awkward accountant, earning a fraction of what he made now. Could he be happy that way? Would it be easier to find love if ginormous dollar signs didn't dominate the landscape and blind everyone?

He didn't want to find love with some random woman. He only wanted Cadence. He should go back in there, put his arm around her, and face the wolves beside her.

Movement behind him and to the side caught his eye.

Cadence strode through the place, head held high, eyes not seeking his. Behind her trailed her parents and then Paul.

Smug, cocky Paul, whose gaze latched onto Graham's unerringly. The guy smirked at him.

Graham balled his hands into fists and forced his butt to remain in the armchair until the entourage had passed.

Should he go find Cadence? But she hadn't even looked his way. Who was he to think she'd appreciate his interference now?

Wasn't there a gym down the north corridor for guests' use?

He'd heard working out was a great stress reliever. And, wow, could he ever use a vent at the moment.

It would have to be later. Now he had to stand by in case Cadence needed him. But how would he know?

CHAPTER TEN

Paisley jumped to her feet when Cadence entered the duplex hours later. "Weston said you took a horse out tonight."

"Yep." And she was still in no mood to talk about it, not that her roommate knew the definition of personal space or private thoughts.

"Which one did you ride?"

Cadence blinked. "Enchantment. He's a bit of a handful, but that was good. Gave me something to focus on." Drat, she'd given Paisley ammunition.

"He's a good one." Paisley studied her. "Have you eaten? I didn't see you in the dining room."

"No. I skipped."

"I bought a box of pizza turnovers last time I was in Jewel Lake. They're in the freezer. Help yourself."

"Bless you." Cadence had been trying to ignore the growling in her belly, trying to convince herself she was so upset that nothing would sit well, anyway. She opened the freezer door and pulled out a couple. "I'll replace these."

Paisley waved her hand in dismissal. "Talking to me will be repayment enough."

Cadence winced. "I should have known."

"Hey, I'm concerned. I saw your parents and your... ex?... in the dining room. He seems like a piece of work."

Ugh. Of course, Paul had made his presence known. Cadence slipped a turnover into the microwave and turned it on before facing her roommate. "They've come up with a new way to trap me. I needed time to think."

"And pray."

"Well, yeah. That, too." But she hadn't done much of either on her ride. Mostly, she'd given Enchantment his head and tried to outrun the tumultuous arguments in her head. It hadn't worked as intended. She'd cantered back into the stable yard at dusk on a sweating gelding to face Weston's grim expression. She'd insisted she could curry Enchantment and settle him herself, and Weston had reluctantly agreed.

Now, Paisley took a seat at the tiny table off their kitchen and pointed Cadence into the other one. "Talk. Start at the beginning."

"I'm twenty-seven years old. That's a long way to go back."

"Funny girl. How did you meet Paul? That's his name, right?"

"I shouldn't have left him to schmooze everyone at Sweet River without me here to defend myself."

"Puh-leeze." Paisley rolled her eyes. "All I can say is he must be a darn good actor who's off his game, because you're way too smart to fall for the narcissistic dude I met tonight."

"I wish that were true." Cadence took a bite of the pizza snack, chewed, and swallowed. "But he can be very charming when he's getting his way."

Paisley grimaced but nodded. "Carry on."

"He was the in thing in college. You know? He had money and looks and…" And what? That was about it, honestly. "Everyone admired him. He was popular and could have dated any girl on campus."

"But he chose you."

"Yeah." She'd never stopped to wonder why. He'd convinced her she was worthy of his attention. Had his parents influenced his choice even that far back? Or had they only taken advantage of it later on, when Cadence and Paul had seemed like an established couple?

Cadence could ask him, but did she want to know? Not badly enough to delve into the past with him. The sooner she rid herself of his slimy attention, the better.

But… would she ever be free of him? The situation seemed impossible. How had Dad managed to become beholden to Daniel Bradley to the point where only the marriage of their kids would clear up the debt? Because there had to be more to it than had come to light this afternoon.

"You're in your head again. Get it out."

Cadence glared at Paisley. "I'm a private person, not one for airing all her dirty laundry in public."

"I'm not the public. I'm your best friend." Paisley's green eyes narrowed as though challenging Cadence to deny the claim. "And you need someone on your side, since it seems Graham Sullivan is too chicken to take that place."

"It's complicated."

"Isn't it always?" Paisley shook her head. "You told me you met Graham in college, too."

"Yeah. He was one of the studious, smart ones, not the partying type like Paul. They're cousins, you know. Their mothers are sisters."

"That's… interesting." Paisley tapped her jaw. "Did you know that then?"

Cadence shrugged. "I probably did, but it was inconsequential. Graham ran in different circles. I wasn't an A student like him, and honestly? I wasn't at school to learn. So even though I bumped into him from time to time, and he seemed aware of me, there wasn't anything to pursue. Not really."

If she could only flip back the calendar by a few years, she'd look at those studious guys differently. She'd think about who would be steadier, who'd be a better champion and father, a better supporter. Not only financially, but of her, as a person.

But all those mistakes? They were hers. They'd formed who she'd become. They'd guided her directly into the mess she found herself in.

"When did you suspect Paul?"

Cadence let out a long sigh. "Never? There was no light-bulb moment. I gradually became aware he didn't truly love me, and I knew I didn't truly love him. But there weren't any huge warning signs."

"Or maybe you ignored them."

"Who's telling this story? Who lived it?"

Paisley mimed zipping her mouth shut and gestured for Cadence to continue.

"Maybe I ignored them, but honestly? There was

nothing big. I heard a couple of rumors he was cheating on me, but he denied those when I asked him. He'd given a coworker a ride home when her car broke down, and they'd stopped for dinner. That sort of thing."

Paisley's face remained expressionless.

"But the marriages around me looked lackluster, too. My parents', for instance. If there'd ever been any passion, it had long dissipated. It seems most people stay married because it's less trouble than separating. There's a kind of co-dependence, but love? Not so much. Have you noticed that?"

"Honestly? I've seen couples like you've mentioned, but I've also seen love that grows and deepens over the years, over the decades. Couples that decided to put each other first."

"I'm sure they exist."

"So I've heard."

Right. Paisley's family was a mess, too. "Look, what would you do, if you were in my boots?"

Paisley's eyebrows shot up. "Lay it on me."

CADENCE'S PARENTS and Paul had sat to one side of the dining hall, largely ignored by everyone else. The resort guests seemed oblivious, which was just as well. Some of the staff had offered a friendly hello, but no one had lingered to chat.

Graham had taken his plate to the office without Nadine batting an eye. It wasn't like it was the first time.

But it was the first time he'd done it simply to avoid unpleasantness in the dining room.

The door opened, and Grandfather peered inside. "I thought I saw a light on in here."

Graham gestured toward his monitor, but it was black. So much for insisting he'd come in here to wrap up a spreadsheet or two.

"Your cousin is an idiot, and the Fosters are no better."

He and Grandfather agreed on that, at least.

"But if you're in here hiding out from them, you're not the man I thought you were."

Graham cringed but tried not to show it.

"At least, if you and Cadence told the truth the day she started working here." Grandfather did not leave that hanging as though it were a question.

"We did, sir. To the best of our knowledge."

"Then why did they pursue her to Montana?"

"You'd have to ask her."

Grandfather's bushy eyebrows hiked. "You're in this room. She is not."

"I don't have all the puzzle pieces, but it sounds like my uncle is holding something over Daniel Foster and will only let it go if Cadence marries Paul."

"What kind of something?"

"That I don't know, sir." Possibly because he'd slithered away rather than face whatever was going on. He'd thought he'd been giving Cadence the space to make her own choices, but in reality, maybe he'd only been proving himself to be the coward he already knew he was.

"Why would that fool want his son in a loveless marriage? Sounds like a hostage situation to me."

"I thought the same thing, sir. I can't imagine why."

Grandfather studied him. "They only ever had the one son. Weren't there miscarriages, as well?"

"I… sir? I'm not privy to that information."

"Daniel Bradley must want his hands on the next generation. That's all I can think of. He'll make a bid for any child Cadence might bear Paul. Then he won't need her anymore."

"But why Cadence? Why not some other woman who might actually love Paul?" Not that Graham could imagine anyone that blind or dull.

"What is Donald Foster's line of business? How does it mesh with Daniel's?"

Graham's brain zipped through the possibilities as though it were a virus-hunting program, but nothing clicked.

"No known mafia connections," Grandfather observed.

Uncle Daniel? Graham blinked. "I haven't heard any rumors to that effect."

"There's something big. There has to be. But, for now, we need to be fully booked by Monday so there's no possibility of this trio extending their stay."

"Uh, we have vacancies…"

"Not anymore, we don't. Put some bogus names on file and charge them to me. They've booked three nights, and we are not allowing them to stay one minute longer."

"Three nights?" Graham hadn't even wondered. His heart sank. He'd let Cadence down. Again.

"One more thing, Graham."

He straightened his back. "Yes, sir?"

"You need to let Cadence know how you feel about her.

You've been moping around for three weeks, and it's getting on my nerves. Just make up your mind and get on with it. That girl needs to be cherished, and I can assure you Paul Bradley has no intention of stepping up to the plate."

Relationship advice from Grandfather? That was rich. On the other hand, their marriage had lasted nearly fifty years and only ended with Grandmother's passing. Even though the man was harsh, he must have been a decent spouse.

Also, the grapevine wasn't as quick around here as Graham had feared, if his grandsire hadn't heard of the kiss to end all kisses seconds before Cadence's guests had arrived.

Kiss to end all kisses? No. Graham definitely didn't want that to be the final one. He wanted a lifetime of them.

But was Cadence free to choose him? Didn't she need space to decide what to do about the ultimatum without Graham's interference? On the other hand, what if she thought she didn't have any other options? What if she felt forced to knuckle under?

That would never do. Not while Graham was alive and able to provide an escape.

"Graham?"

He shook his head slightly and focused on Grandfather. "You might be right, sir."

"I'm always right."

Sure. Except when he was wrong which, admittedly, wasn't very often. "I'll keep that in mind."

Was humor glinting in the old man's eyes? That definitely didn't show too often.

"You're well able to provide for a wife and a family, boy. Sometimes a man has to stick his neck out to lay a claim on what he wants. It's not always easy being male, not in this day of women's lib."

Women's lib had been a thing long before Graham was born, but he guessed he could see the landscape had changed since a youthful Walter Sullivan had an affair with his pretty, young secretary. "Are you ever planning on meeting up with Eleanor?" he blurted.

Grandfather reared back. "Why would I do that? Nadine says her mother doesn't want to talk to me."

"Maybe I get my cowardice from you."

The man's eyes narrowed. "Watch your tongue."

"I see a similarity. You need closure, and so does she, if she'd only admit it. I'm not saying you need to marry the woman—"

Grandfather harrumphed and jammed his crossed arms over his chest.

"—but offering a sincere, in-person apology might not go amiss."

"What has that got to do with you?"

Graham took a deep breath. "I'll pray for you if you pray for me."

"I pray for you every day already, boy."

"You do?"

"Of course, I do. You're my grandson. You're my employee. I couldn't run this place without you."

"You couldn't?"

"What's wrong with your ears? Your eyes? Look around you. Who could do a better job of collating all the Sullivan numbers? No one, that's who. I depend on you. I need you to be settled and content, so go find Cadence and get started on that."

"When are you calling Eleanor?"

Grandfather rolled his eyes. "Back to that, are we? There's no relationship."

"We can both be brave. Together." That would get him off the hook, right? Because there was no way the old man was going to reverse decades of conditioning.

Did Graham want to be off the hook? No, not really, but he didn't want to be pushed, either. So much that he allowed others to push Cadence because of his reluctance?

No. He needed to step up, either way.

But so did his grandsire.

"You drive a hard bargain. I'll talk to Nadine about it in the morning. Is that good enough for you?"

Graham blinked in astonishment. "Uh, yes, sir. Definitely good enough for now."

"You, on the other hand..." The old man's shrewd eyes assessed him. "You have no such excuse. Cadence is right here on this ranch— somewhere — and she needs a champion. A knight in shining armor, if you will."

"Then I'm the wrong guy, because I'm no kind of hero." Did women today even want to have some guy swoop in and rescue them?

"Nonsense. You're the right one. You just need to get yourself a backbone, and the only way I know to do that is to commit your way to the Lord and let Him direct your path."

Sometimes the old man made a lot of sense.

"You can follow your cousin's example — Tate, that is, not Paul — and build here on the ranch or make your home in Chicago. But get off your rear and do something about that girl."

"Yes, sir."

Wait, how had he agreed? Conditioning. What Grandfather decreed got an automatic salute.

"What are you waiting for?"

"Pardon?"

"Get up! Quit hiding in this office. Go find your woman."

"Tonight?"

"Why not?"

Uh, Graham could think of a thousand reasons, and at least one of them would stick. He was too chicken.

CHAPTER ELEVEN

G ood afternoon, son." Mother air-kissed both sides of Graham's face.

"Good afternoon. Did you have a nice flight?" Graham looked between his parents and his uncle and aunt.

"Two flights, since we were required to fly via Kansas to pick up Maribel." Mother rolled her eyes.

Uncle James cast a surly look at his ex-wife. "It's time Father moved our board meetings back to Chicago. All this extra time in the air takes hours away from the business end of things."

Dad nodded and turned to Graham. "I'm sure you can't wait to be back in the city again, as well, son. Help us apply some pressure to the old man. I have no idea why he's insisting on hanging out in the middle of nowhere. Back in April, it sounded like it would be two or three months, tops, and here we are, four months in, and he seems more entrenched than ever."

Hmm. Was Grandfather trying to outwait Nadine's

mother? Maybe. But Graham wasn't going to mention it. Not to this group.

"It certainly isn't convenient to come to Montana this often," Aunt Maribel agreed. "Now that Walter has put Tate in charge of this venture — I still can't believe my son offered to live onsite indefinitely — Walter isn't needed here anymore. Now it seems he's just being stubborn." She lowered her voice. "Have there been other signs he's declining mentally?"

"Grandfather?" Graham couldn't have stopped the incredulous laugh had he tried. "Trust me. There's nothing wrong with his mind. He's as sharp as ever."

Uncle James sighed.

Did the man want his father to decline? Was he tired of waiting to take over Sullivan Enterprises? Graham couldn't see it. The tension between Uncle James and Dad wouldn't subside at their father's death, unless... did they plan to divide the empire? How would that work, anyway? James had three kids, and Dad only one. And then there was Grandfather's daughter, Nadine, and her two sons. Surely, Grandfather's estate would be fair to each of his offspring.

Had the old man had time to rewrite his will with Nadine, Weston, and Jude in mind? If he planned to leave Sweet River Ranch to that branch of the family, he wouldn't have named Tate as CEO, would he?

"*Paul?* What's my nephew doing here?" Mom's eyes sharpened as she looked past Graham.

This was no time to be woolgathering. Not when they stood along the fringes of the lodge's great room in full sight of any guests, including Graham's least favorite cousin.

"Aunt Bridget!" Paul approached, kissed Mom's cheek, then tossed a cocky wink in Graham's direction. "Did Gray forget to mention I was here?"

"He definitely failed in that regard."

And nearly every other area of life, it seemed at times. And his name was Graham, thanks very much.

"I'm sure you heard Cadence and I postponed our wedding, but I've come to get everything back on track. Daniel and Amelia are here, as well."

"Postponed?" The word shot out of Graham's mouth. "That's not the way I heard the story."

"Your ears are stuffed full of... cotton."

Mom patted Paul's arm. "I hope it all works out for you. Cadence is such a lovely girl."

"She sure is," Paul agreed with a smirk.

Traitors, both of them. Dad and Uncle James had already drifted a few feet away to confer in low tones, and only Aunt Maribel studied Graham thoughtfully. He was going to have to pull his mom aside and explain a few things to her. Like that he was in love with Cadence?

He was, wasn't he? But he could hardly proclaim that to anyone until the Fosters and Paul had given up their fools' quest and returned to Chicago. For all Grandfather's push last night, Graham wasn't quite ready to stick his neck out while Paul was around to give it a chop.

Enough. Graham brushed his hands together. "Well, let's get everyone settled. I believe Grandfather has planned a family get-together this evening, then a full day of board meetings tomorrow."

"Family get-together," Dad muttered. "I suppose he's including his illegitimate offspring in that."

"I'm sure he is." Graham kept his voice as pleasant as possible.

Paul guffawed. "I couldn't believe it when I heard that rumor. You're telling me it's true? The old man has another kid?"

Dad inhaled sharply and skewered his nephew with a deadly look, not that Paul noticed.

Graham had thought it was awkward having Uncle James and Aunt Maribel in the same space, but it was a familiar form of discomfort. Adding Paul to the mix was like tossing a hand grenade into a fire that had been somewhat contained previously.

"Welcome to Sweet River Ranch!" Grandfather's bright voice came from behind them. "Good flights?"

Never had Graham been so glad to see the older man. Let him handle his messy family.

After kissing Mom and Aunt Maribel and shaking hands with Dad and Uncle James, Grandfather pinned his gaze on Paul. "Is there something I can help you with, young man? Any rumors you'd like to discuss with me?"

Paul retreated a half-step. "No, sir. Everything is fine, sir."

"I suggest you find a flight back to Chicago very soon. The lodge here seems to be overbooked this coming weekend, and I'd hate for you to find yourself sleeping in the stable."

Paul's gaze shifted. "I'll look into flights, sir."

"Excellent." Grandfather turned back to Uncle James and Dad. "Shall we step aside?"

The brothers nodded and closed ranks around their father as they walked away, the women right behind them.

Paul glowered at Graham. "You think you're really somebody with Walter Sullivan for a grandfather, don't you?"

There had certainly been times when Graham had held his head high on that account, but he'd come to realize that it was an advantage he'd done nothing to deserve. "I've been blessed," he replied simply.

Paul snorted, sidled closer, and lowered his voice. "You think Cadence is going to fall all over you because you can rescue her from this mess her father put her in? She won't. She doesn't dare."

Graham's gut tightened. "You don't love her, so why not let her go graciously?"

"It's not up to me."

"Sure, it is."

"Nope. I'd release her — again — if I could, but I'm kind of over a barrel here, same as her. It's a thing with our fathers and their companies." His cousin shrugged. "It can't be helped, but we only need to stay married for two or three years. I'm willing to make the sacrifice for the good of Bradley Consortium."

"For money, you mean."

"Well, yeah. You'd do the same."

"I don't think so."

"If you had it in your power to keep your old man's business from going belly-up and taking your own fortune with it? I'm pretty sure you'd do what you could."

"Not if it included ruining someone else's life."

"Ruin?" Paul laughed harshly. "I'm not that bad. She can give me a son, whom I'll retain custody of in the divorce settlement. I guess if she wants access, she'll stick around longer, but she'll probably be glad to be rid of any reminders of me. Not that I plan on being abusive or anything like that. Just... I get that I'm not her favorite person at the moment, and that's not likely to change."

If Graham slugged his cousin, he'd be on the hard floor calling uncle in seconds. Still, the temptation had never been stronger. He clenched his fists. Clenched his jaw.

Paul smirked. "And you can be there to pick up the pieces, cousin. All's fair in love and war, right?"

Graham pivoted on his heel and strode away.

CADENCE BECAME aware of Paisley's long fingernails piercing the skin of her forearm.

"Did you hear that?" Paisley hissed in her ear.

Oh, had she ever. Cadence and her roommate had come into the lodge just in time to overhear Paul's not-so-veiled threat. Now she grabbed Paisley's arm and pivoted for the door.

"Go over there, and tell him off!"

"No." Red rage nearly blinded her. It definitely wasn't that she didn't want to flay Paul, verbally or otherwise. It was that she refused to make a scene, but maybe the time had come.

Cadence was too malleable. She'd taken the easy way far too many times. Look at her dating history. Look at her relationship with Paul. Look at how she'd latched onto Graham's offer without a second thought.

She'd been alternating between pretending she had no

problems and running from them, always taking the path of least resistance. That stopped now.

Graham huffed away down the corridor to the office wing. Paul began to turn, and Cadence yanked Paisley behind a tall potted plant before he could see her.

Okay, maybe her evasion would stop later. She couldn't flip a switch and blast Paul without any forethought. Too much was at stake.

Were her parents actually in danger of losing everything if Cadence didn't marry Paul? It didn't seem possible. And Paul — despicable, horrid man — thought he could get her pregnant, take the baby — what if it was a girl? what if she didn't conceive? — and abandon Cadence? The absolute nerve of his egotistical, narcissistic—

"Cadence?"

She blinked hard and turned to her roommate. "Yes?"

"The line is forming for dinner. Are we eating or not?"

"You may. I think I'm heading back to the duplex."

"We ate the last of the pizza pops for snack last night."

"Right." Cadence gritted her teeth. She hated going hungry. She also hated feeling like the coward she was. "Fine, we can stay, but don't let that man anywhere near me."

And now she was making her roommate take responsibility. *Grow up, Cadence. Face your own problems.*

"There are two spaces at the staff table with Weston, Jude, Kaci, and Tyler. Go hold those, and I'll get two plates."

Paul wouldn't dare take on surly Weston. Neither would Graham, should he bother to return. Or possibly the Sullivans were having an elite dinner in their suites and hadn't bothered to invite the Kline grandsons. Whatever. "Sure. Thanks. I owe you."

"Oh, don't worry. I fully plan to collect." Paisley winked and gave her a little shove. "I'll be right back. Go make nice."

"Yeah, yeah." Cadence put purpose in her step as she wended between the tables. She slid into one of the two vacant chairs. "Were these saved for someone else? Paisley has gone to grab our food."

"Saved for you." Kaci grinned. "I hear you've met up with a little drama the past couple of days."

Cadence gritted her teeth. "Far too much." And all of it far too public.

Weston studied her. "Need to take Enchantment out again?"

What, had she won the mighty cowboy over with her equine skills? "Not tonight, I think." The wind in her hair and the power of the horse between her knees had offered some comfort last night, but she hadn't taken the time she needed to still her mind. She had a feeling her life, her future, depended on her relationship with God. One she'd coasted along with, much as she'd slid along with the rest of her life's decisions.

No more. She had to take control. No, she had to hand control over to God. Or something. She needed time. Prayer. Clear-headedness in the midst of all these swirling emotions and demands.

Cadence looked around the table and evaluated those present. They were all believers, weren't they? They'd been in church most Sundays. "Can I ask you guys to pray for me? I have some difficult decisions to make."

"I'm happy to pray for you." Kaci glanced toward the tables that Cadence had her back to. "But I'm not sure you need to pray about that annoying ex of yours. Keep him exed. He's a loser."

If only it were that simple. "There's a lot more than meets the eye."

Jude laughed. "Are you trying to tell us he's a nice guy under all that bluster? Because I'm not seeing it."

"No." Cadence exhaled. "That's not what I mean. There's an entire… situation."

Weston narrowed his eyes and studied her.

What was the cowboy reading on her face? Cadence kept her expression as impassive as possible and sighed with relief when Paisley set a tray down on the table and began unloading bowls of chili and plates of cornbread. "Thanks."

"You're welcome." Paisley slid into the chair between Cadence and Weston and pointed her spoon at Weston. "Your mother makes the best chili I've ever tasted."

The guy nearly smiled. "She's a good cook."

"I've never eaten better in my life."

Paisley had told Cadence about the loser parents she had and all the drugs that had been in her home growing up, so maybe Nadine didn't have much competition. But, on the other hand, Cadence's parents could afford the best, and she still had to agree that Nadine's food was mighty fine.

Could her parents still afford the best if Cadence turned Paul down for good? Her gut soured. Why did she even think about that with an *if* in the middle? She couldn't in good conscience marry the poser. And why was it her responsibility to save her parents from financial ruin when it was them, not her, who'd made a sketchy deal with Donald Bradley?

But then there was that whole *honor your father and mother* thing. How far did that go?

Paisley nudged her elbow. "Here's the butter for your cornbread."

"Right. Thanks."

Was there any way Cadence could sort through all this on her own, or did she need counseling? And where, on this remote ranch with only a hick town nearby, would she find someone she could trust?

Lord? I need help. All the help.

If only He'd drop clarity into her lap, into her mind, with no doubts remaining. That couldn't be too much to ask, could it?

CHAPTER TWELVE

Graham had been watching for Cadence to return to the duplex she shared with Paisley for so long he'd begun to wonder if they had a back door he didn't know about. The solar-powered streetlights glowed before the two of them turned onto Hummingbird Lane.

He levered off his front porch. "Cadence? Can we talk?"

The two women paused, but their faces were in the shadows.

"Please?"

"Not tonight."

But why was Paisley answering? "Cadence?"

"It's been a long day, Graham."

Wow, she sounded exhausted. Graham got it. He would be, too. In fact, he was. "Okay." He wanted to talk about the kiss. Talk about what Paul had said afterward. Tell her he loved her and wanted to fix everything for her.

Ask her to marry him.

Yeah, premature. He knew it, but still.

Maybe it was as well Paisley was protecting Cadence. Right now, she was tugging Cadence's arm, encouraging her to keep walking.

One amazing kiss hadn't earned him the right to interfere. But he'd also rescued her in Chicago. No, she didn't owe him anything for that. They needed to talk — without him pressuring her or making assumptions — and that wouldn't be tonight.

"See you tomorrow?"

Cadence nodded. Turned away.

He hated how needy he sounded, but... he was. She was the one who'd come to find him earlier today. She was the one who'd kissed him like there was no tomorrow.

Like there was no tomorrow.

Desperation clawed up his throat as the duo turned in at their own lodging. Had that kiss been a goodbye of sorts? He'd looked at is as a beginning, not an end. He replayed her words. Had he misunderstood?

The women's door clicked shut, and an interior light turned a curtain-covered window into a glowing rectangle.

There was a metaphor there, it seemed. There was light, but sight was occluded. That summed up his relationship with Cadence to a tee. Just enough light for a glimmer of hope. Not enough to see clearly.

She showed just the glimpses she wanted to show via social media. Yeah, he kept an eye on the Sweet River accounts, trying to learn more about her.

Graham was a simple man. He was clever with numbers and obtuse with people. Always had been.

A bat swooped through the beam of the streetlight. A loon called from the lake. Something rustled in the bushes across the lane. His surroundings were nothing like Chicago. He'd never have dared sit outside absorbing the night air there. Maybe if he had a penthouse with a rooftop patio like Tate's, but Graham had never been outdoorsy.

Montana was growing on him. Sort of.

Footsteps sounded on the lane, and he turned to see which staff member was returning now. Weston. Great. Graham should have gone inside already.

"Hey there. Nice night."

"Hi, Weston."

The cowboy paused in about the same spot the women had, which meant Weston's face was as shadowed as Cadence's had been. "It's nice the mosquitoes seem to have died off."

"Yes." Graham hadn't even thought of that. In June, he'd been too busy smacking bugs to stay out like this.

"You doing okay?"

Graham blinked. Since when was Weston concerned about anyone other than himself? "I've been better."

"I bet. That Paul dude is your cousin, huh?"

"Do I have to own up to it? He's a jerk."

The cowboy snorted. "We don't get to pick our relatives, just our friends."

"True." Weston's words had been heavy with meaning. Maybe it was time Graham extended an olive branch. "Paul is my least favorite cousin of all time."

"Worse than me and Jude? That's saying something."

"It's not like what happened between my grandfather and your grandmother was your fault any more than it was mine."

"Yeah. We had a bit more warning than you guys did

about what was coming down, though. We've known all our lives we must have more family out there somewhere."

"While we had no clue."

"Bit of a shock, huh?"

"No kidding."

"I'd like to say sorry, but…" Weston's voice drifted off as his hands spread to the sides.

"But it's not your fault." The guy had been plenty rude, but had Graham and the other cousins been any better? "I'm sorry for not being nicer."

"Yeah. No prob."

Graham still wasn't sure he wanted to be best friends, though. He pulled to his feet. "It's been a long day, and tomorrow doesn't look like it will be any shorter."

"Want some free advice?"

No? Also, he didn't want paid advice.

"You Sullivans talk a lot about God. About praying."

Graham stilled. "Yes?"

"But do you actually do it? I don't mean any offense. I'm only observing. There's talk, and then there's action."

"We are honestly seeking God's direction and trying to follow it."

"Okay."

But Weston's voice didn't sound like he believed Graham. "Why do you ask?"

The guy shrugged. "Your grandpa just barrels right along with his plans. Hard to believe he's so in tune with God no course correction is ever needed."

"He's your grandfather, too." Stupid thing to say. It was like Graham was avoiding the point.

"Yeah, well. My other grandpa took me fishing and

taught me to ride and a whole lot of nature lore. Seems a mite more friendly than a dude who sits at the head of a conference table who blasts everyone and throws his weight and his dollars around."

The nerve. Graham clenched his fists and gritted his teeth. Why should he defend Grandfather to Weston Kline? Walter Sullivan was a good man, a whole lot nicer than his mother's dad, who'd died of heart failure years ago. Graham's few memories were of a red-faced man cursing in his native Icelandic tongue.

It was a wonder Mom had turned out as well as she had, actually. Paul's mother, Aunt Frances, seemed to take more after their father.

"Nothing to say?" Weston taunted.

Graham's attention refocused on his newfound cousin. "There's more to Grandfather than meets the eye."

"Right. The dude knocked up his secretary."

"That's not what I meant, but okay. He's human. I'm not excusing what he did, but that's evidence he hasn't always sought God's will in everything he does. I can't deny he's on the controlling side, but he's worked hard to make Sullivan Enterprises even greater than what he inherited from his own father. He's changed with the times. How many eighty-year-olds do you know who are as technology literate as he is?"

"I don't know many eighty-year-olds."

Did that require a response? While Graham deliberated, Weston went on.

"But my seventy-five-year-old grandmother has no use for any of it. Mom bought her a cell phone, and Nana got all flustered and said she didn't need it. The box on the wall had done her fine all her life and would continue to do so. No need for a pocket-size device that thought it was smarter than she was."

"Right." Graham managed a chuckle. "That's probably more typical."

"But you didn't answer my question. About God."

"You're a Christian, right?"

"Yeah? But then I'm not pretending to be perfect."

"Who is?"

Weston snorted. "All of you. Holier-than-thou and all that."

"I don't think—"

"Never mind. I shouldn't have expected you might be open to hearing what other people see."

"But I am."

"Forget it." Weston laughed. "It's too complicated for a math nerd like you."

Graham opened his mouth. Closed it. Watched his cousin saunter away. And knew he'd be thinking on what Weston had said.

He talked faith. But did the rubber meet the road?

"He can't make you do it, you know."

Cadence took a long breath and turned to face her roommate. "Can't he?"

"Of course not. If he at least turned on the charm and pretended he loved you, I could see a girl *maybe* falling for that. But he tipped his hand." Paisley snorted. "Seriously, what kind of medieval lord does he think he is, laying claim to your firstborn and then dismissing you?"

"But my parents…"

"Do you think they'd willingly give up their only grand-child to the likes of Paul and his family? No. I'm guessing they don't know this angle. Talk to them."

It seemed a long shot. Paul seemed to have her parents firmly in his pocket. Paisley had a point, though. Mom had hinted often enough that she'd like to spoil her grandchil-dren before she died of old age.

But talk to them? Lay it out? First, she'd have to get them away from Paul. And then hope and pray he hadn't poisoned them too deeply for them to see her side. But Mom remembered being poor as the child of Icelandic immigrants. The trappings of the life she lived as Daniel Foster's wife wouldn't be willingly given up.

"You need legal counsel. Know any lawyers?"

Cadence managed a sharp laugh. "Graham's mother, Bridget."

"There you go. She's even here right now. Seems an intimidating woman, but whatever. I guess that comes with being a lawyer."

"Don't you get it? Graham's mother and Paul's mother are sisters."

"Right, I forgot." Paisley deflated. "Are they close?"

"Does it matter? Blood runs thicker than water. There would be a conflict of interest at the very least."

"Because of the *interest* you have in Graham."

Cadence shook her head. "I was. I'd like to be. But this is all too complicated, and I can't drag him into it. He's too… trusting."

Paisley's eyebrows shot up. "You mean gullible? You don't think he'd fight for you?"

"He shouldn't have to, speaking of medieval. Women are perfectly capable of wielding their own swords these days and slaying their own dragons."

"Then slay away already."

"I don't know how." The tension in Cadence's gut threatened to boil over.

"Do you even hear yourself?"

"What?"

"Look, the guy came to your rescue once already. He—"

"I know. I took advantage of him."

"That's not how you told the story initially. He made the offer. All you did was take him up on it. How's that taking advantage of him?"

"I didn't give him a chance to think it through. We left Chicago in the middle of the night."

"Puh-leeze."

"What?"

"He's a grownup. I've known him for what, three months now? He's quiet. Not very outdoorsy. But he's genuine. I wouldn't have bagged him as impulsive."

"He's not." Except he had been. What to think?

Paisley gave a firm nod. "Exactly."

"It's been a long day. I'm not following."

"In all this time, I've only seen Graham Sullivan do one impulsive thing, and that was return a few days earlier than planned with a jilted bride in tow."

Cadence flinched. "Thanks for the reminder."

"So... was he being impulsive? Or wasn't he?"

"He didn't come to Chicago expecting to rescue me,

that's for sure. He didn't know I needed it." She hadn't known it herself, but she should have. If only she hadn't stuck her ostrich head in the sand and, instead, kept a keen lookout around her.

"Therefore, I deduce that his rescuer side is more prominent than his deliberate side. It just doesn't get called on every day, but when it does, look out, world."

Was her roommate right? It made sense. Taken to a logical conclusion — if she were even capable of one after the excessively emotional, long day she'd had — it was no wonder Graham had backed off once she was settled at the ranch. His job was done. She was rescued, and he could go back to his carefully curated, methodical life with a clear conscience.

There was no room for wild cards like Cadence Foster in a life like that.

And she'd kissed him like a wanton woman, practically assaulting him in the process. Had she given him a chance to say no? Not so much.

Cadence looked over to where Paisley sat in the easy chair, a smug grin on her face. "You're right."

"Always."

"And modest."

Paisley chuckled. "So, you'll talk to Graham tomorrow, like you promised?"

"If I don't chicken out."

"I'll pray for you."

"Thanks. I need it." Because it wasn't going to be easy to apologize to Graham and acknowledge that she'd taken advantage of his inability to leave a damsel wallowing in her distress.

But she needed to face it. She needed to take responsibility for her own actions. She needed to rescue herself without Graham's help, even when it felt like Paul had tightened his grip on her wrist and wasn't about to let go.

The guys might be cousins, but the situation wasn't Graham's fault nor his problem. He didn't need to keep extricating her from difficulties she'd brought upon herself.

It was up to her. She took a deep breath and imagined herself tugging up her big-girl panties.

God helped those who helped themselves, right? That was in the Bible somewhere. She couldn't quite remember where, but she'd heard it often enough, so it must be true.

So, she'd find her way through this mess with Paul, hopefully without ruining her parents' lives in the process, and then God could bless her. If she could ask a boon, it would be that the blessing would include Graham.

Boon. Who talked like that? Only people in fantasy novels. No one in this millennium, that was for sure.

CHAPTER THIRTEEN

C adence hadn't been at breakfast, and Graham couldn't wait any longer. Not when Grandfather's meeting would start in five minutes in the conference room. He didn't dare be late for that.

Aunt Nadine wiped her hands on her apron as she passed Graham, offering a smile.

He smiled back and fell into step beside her. "You're brave."

"Me?" She laughed. "I'm shaking in my boots."

Graham glanced down at her sensible white tennis shoes.

"Metaphorically."

"The Sullivans don't bite."

"Someday I might believe you. Today is not that day." She tilted up her chin and swept into the conference room ahead of him.

Graham paused in the doorway. Graham's parents and aunt and uncle flanked the head of the table, where Grandfather scrolled on his phone, ignoring everyone. Jude poured a coffee for Aunt Nadine, while Tate and his brothers took their seats.

The only space left was between Dad and Weston.

Fine. Graham could sit there. The grouchy cowboy might think he had insights into the clan, but Graham could ignore his opinions for the time being. Mostly, he needed to survive this meeting so he could find Cadence. He wanted — needed — to tell her how much she meant to him. How he wanted to stand by her side for the rest of their lives.

No matter how often he told himself it was way too early to declare himself to her, he kept circling back. Which didn't make it the right move.

Weston had accused him — he'd accused the entire family, really — of saying the right words to God but then doing what they wanted, anyway, without listening for a reply.

Seriously, how long did a person need to wait when the right answer was obvious and smack dab in front of him?

Weston leaned toward him as he sat down, stroking his chin. "Nice look," he whispered with a smirk.

Now the guy was making fun of Graham's attempt at growing a beard? Graham glared at him and flipped open his laptop.

When everyone had taken seats, Grandfather set his phone down and clasped his hands in front of him on the table. His gaze took in each person individually: Uncle James, Dad, Graham, Weston, Jude, then Aunt Nadine on the end, then back up the other side of the table: Bryce, Maxwell, Tate, Aunt Maribel, and Mom. "Thank you for coming."

Graham managed to hold the snort in, but a surreptitious glance at Weston revealed a quick smirk. Apparently, the newest clan members found Grandfather's controlling nature off-putting. Well, they didn't have to be here. The Sullivans had managed fine all these years — decades, even — without the Klines.

Conscience jabbed. Maybe the Klines hadn't fared as well. Maybe they deserved to be here as much as the Sullivans. But why did Weston need to waffle between annoyance and amusement? Couldn't the cowboy simply be grateful to be included as a rightful heir without judging everything?

Grandfather began his meeting with a scripture and a word of prayer.

Was this ritual what Weston had accused? Simply a way to sugarcoat Sullivan Enterprises and make it palatable to God?

Graham studied the relatives around the table. Every one of them would claim to be a believer, but how many of them actually lived like it on a minute-to-minute basis?

Did Graham?

Not if Weston were to be believed. But how did that dude get off on making Graham doubt his relationship with God? The Sullivans were a decisive bunch. You didn't get to this level in the hotel industry without a broad understanding of how business worked... or without the ability to pivot at a moment's notice.

Mom had complained time and again that Graham thought everything to the death and, here he was, doing it again. He refocused on Grandfather as the old man briefed the family on the recent acquisition of Cassel Hotels, a boutique chain with a dozen locations around Lake Michigan.

Tate had inked that deal a few weeks ago. Good old Tate. Graham's cousin deserved to be CEO of Sweet River Ranch and to be a valued part of upper management alongside the older generation.

The primary chain was also doing well. Grandfather pulled some numbers and commended Uncle James for the minimal downtime a recent fire had caused in their Milwaukee hotel.

Graham stifled a yawn. So far, there wasn't anything that couldn't have been handled easily via video conference. And it wasn't like Grandfather was afraid of the technology. The man might be eighty, but he'd embraced the digital era like he'd been born to it.

Grandfather tapped his phone, likely to slide down his meeting agenda. "Sweet River Ranch." He looked up and scanned the group. "We're holding our own here. There have been some major expenditures aside from acquiring the property. Maxwell is busy spending every penny I've allotted for renovations and upkeep."

Across the table, Max shifted in his chair with an awkward grin. He'd been running a profitable business flipping properties before Grandfather had pulled him to the ranch.

Grandfather glanced at his notes. "The cottages on Dragonfly Lane only required refreshing. They were outfitted with new linens and draperies. They've been keeping at about 80% booked since we opened Memorial Day."

The lakeshore cottages looked inviting. Graham would give the crew that.

"Firefly Lane is nearly complete. Those cabins are fully booked through August, with some reservations into the fall." Grandfather looked up. "The previous owners had begun renovations there, but they'd honestly left quite a mess. They'd also started to build on Ladybug Lane. Max's crew will shift there next. We plan to have those ready for next spring."

Nothing new, so far.

"As you know, Tate and Stephanie are planning to build on the corner of Hummingbird Lane. That offer extends to every one of you, should you wish to make Sweet River your permanent home."

Why was Grandfather looking at him like that? Graham shifted in his seat. He was a city boy, remember? He wasn't sticking around Montana any longer than he needed to. Right?

Except the rural quiet was getting to him in a positive way. He didn't miss the hustle, the sirens, the people in his face everywhere he went.

Mountain lions. Grizzly bears. Rattlesnakes. Mosquitoes. He needed to remember all the downsides of living in the Wild West. Not that he'd seen any of those creatures, other than the pesky little bloodsuckers, but they existed. He knew they did. Weston had told him horror stories about those and more. Skunks. Wolves.

Would Weston pull his leg? Sheesh, that was a distinct possibility, but he hadn't in this case. Graham had looked the wildlife up, and they definitely were native to this region.

Would Cadence want to stay in Montana? What was drawing her back to Chicago? Not her parents, certainly. Not a job. She seemed to love it here.

For the first time, Graham caught a glimmer of understanding for why Tate had pivoted and chosen the ranch as his home. If it made Stephanie happy, it made Tate happy. Wasn't that how marriage should work?

Some things couples needed to compromise on, but their place of residence wasn't one of those, unless they spent six months in each location. Hmm.

"Graham suggested treehouses as a future option. Apparently, there are tourists looking for experiences like that."

Graham straightened, blinking. Since when had Grandfather taken his recommendation seriously? He'd turned in the rudimentary proposal Grandfather had asked for after their brainstorming session in April, but he hadn't heard a thing until this minute.

"I have a team of architects looking into the possibility. We've identified a location on the riverbank we'll call Eagles Nest that might make sense for a cluster of treehouses around a common restroom area." Grandfather shook his head. "Why anyone would rather sleep up in the trees than have an ensuite beats me, but it's a thing. They'll even pay more for the privilege of climbing up and down a ladder to use the facilities. Give me a private jetted tub any day of the week."

Interesting. The old man preferred baths to showers? Graham filed that information.

Grandfather leaned back and surveyed his offspring. "I'd like to hear your thoughts on treehouses and

Conestoga wagons and yurts, as they all fall into a similar style called glamping."

Well. Old dogs could be taught new tricks, after all. Never in a million years had Graham thought Grandfather would take his offhand suggestion seriously. Honestly? It had been the only thing he could think of at the time to contribute to the conversation at all.

"IT SEEMS WE'VE WASTED A TRIP." Dad glowered at Cadence.

Mom wrung her hands, but were those tears glimmering on the ends of her impossibly long eyelashes real or fake?

Cadence had thought she knew her mother, but she'd been wrong. She braced herself. "I can't marry Paul. I'm truly sorry you're in financial difficulty because of it, but I refuse to be your sacrificial lamb."

"We invested a lot of money into this wedding." Dad wasn't giving an inch.

"I'll pay you back."

He scoffed. "With what? How much is Walter Sullivan paying you to run social media pages?" Dad's disdain was clear. "Minimum wage isn't going to get you very far."

It was considerably more than minimum wage, but Cadence would chew her own lips off before divulging the amount. It wasn't any of Dad's business. Except it kind of was.

Ack, the guilt over canceling everything at the last minute. "I'll consult an accountant—" Graham's face materialized in her mind, and she banished him "—and set up a payment plan."

"That's not going to cut it, Cadence. Not unless you are talking about thousands a month. Tens of thousands would be better."

She stared at him. Just how much trouble was his business in? But she steeled herself. If he'd gambled everything to the point where only a connection with Donald Bradley could save him, that wasn't her problem.

It was in her power to save her parents. Shouldn't a good daughter do that?

But not by marrying a creep who didn't love her. This wasn't Victorian England or some fantasy world that operated on a similar premise of advantageous marriages solving everyone's problems.

All she knew of those, she'd read in fiction, and romance had made the sacrifices palatable. Nothing could make a union with Paul Bradley agreeable. She shuddered at the thought of welcoming his touch.

So. Not. Happening.

"I can't believe the nerve of Walter threatening Paul if he didn't leave this godforsaken ranch today." Dad paced their guest room. "We paid the ridiculous resort fee to stay here for two more nights."

That was the best news Cadence had had in the past couple of days. "You don't have to leave because Paul does."

Her father sighed heavily. "Of course, we do. You aren't giving us anything to work with here, Cadence. We have affairs to set in order at home."

She eyed him. "Have you been gambling?"

He reared back, his eyes narrowing on her. "What made you think of that?"

It had been a shot in the dark, but a few random memories had coalesced into something that made sense. "Have you?"

Ramrod stiff, Mom stared down at the hands clenched in her lap.

"How I manage my business is none of yours."

"Except, you've made it my business by gambling on me."

Mom's shoulders quivered.

Maybe she was the one who'd been indiscreet? Who'd gotten their finances in a twist? "When you get home, please make copies of the invoices you'd like me to help with, and I'll do the best I can as soon as possible."

"Too little, too late." Dad's hand sliced through the air. "We need for all this to go away. We need you married to Paul weeks ago. Be thankful he's sorry for breaking things off and is willing to reconsider."

"Because you've got him over the same barrel you've got me. How did this issue with Bradley Consortium become a problem for your kids' generation?" If only she could wipe away the guilt of her part in their financial difficulties. If only they hadn't laid out so much for her wedding. She hadn't asked for it — not much, anyway — but it was still her problem.

Would Walter Sullivan loan her the money she needed? She might be working for him forever to repay him, but that had to be better than dealing with her parents.

She could ask him. She just needed numbers.

Numbers went through the accounting department.

Graham saw every single one of them. Logged them into tidy columns.

Maybe she could ask Mr. Sullivan to keep their discussion private. He was astute. He'd understand.

Because Graham would probably think the solution would be to marry her and save her from her poor choices. From her parents' poor choices.

Being married to Graham would be amazing, but not because he felt sorry for her. She'd been running from one difficulty to another ever since that June evening, while Graham patiently stood by, extricating her from the results, time and time again.

To let him rescue her once more was no better than marrying Paul. Oh, Graham was a way nicer guy, but he deserved better. He deserved a woman who could come to marriage as an equal, not as a project.

Maybe one day that would be her, but not right now. Not when it seemed she stood on quicksand and anyone standing with her was destined to sink along with her.

CHAPTER FOURTEEN

Dad skewered Graham with a look. "What is this nonsense about clapping?"

Graham blinked. "Clapping?"

"You know. The treehouses and wagons." Dad shook his head "I haven't heard anything more ridiculous in a long time."

"The word is glamping, a blend between glamorous and camping."

"What's glamorous about not having an ensuite?"

"The glamor comes from the rest of it. It's honestly a thing people are looking for in a vacation."

"It's dumb."

"It's a way for Sweet River Ranch to stand out and lure in tourists who are looking for something a little bit different than a lakeside cottage or lodge that offers horse-back riding."

"There's already a campground. Some people even sleep in *tents*."

When had Dad become so snooty? Perhaps he always had been. Perhaps Graham had been the same, but working at the ranch with a wide variety of staff and visitors, most of them not as privileged as he was, had opened his eyes. At least a bit.

Yeah, he was aware that everyone knew which were the Sullivan grandsons and how they were in charge. It put his cousins and him a cut above the rest, but he'd begun to see the others as regular people. Kaci, for instance. Heather, on Maxwell's construction crew. Tyler, over in the stable.

But the longer he rubbed elbows with such a varied crew, he was coming to realize they weren't intrinsically different.

Cadence had known that all along. She'd seemed content from the beginning to live with Paisley, her only comment being how much Paisley talked. Now, it seemed, they spent a lot of time together.

"Graham? Speak to the old man."

He refocused on his father. "I don't think you need to worry about treehouses or yurts at any of the Sullivan hotels. We're doing something different here at the resort. It's a distinctive clientele, and that's okay."

"While you're talking to him, get his permission to return to the Chicago office. I'm afraid the air out here is getting to you."

"The air?" Graham straightened his spine. "I'll be back in the office when Grandfather is ready to release me. He knows what he's doing."

Dad rolled his eyes. "If you ask me, he's sliding off his rocking chair, bit by bit."

"You're wrong. He's as sharp as ever."

"This whole affair has derailed him."

"It's made him more human. He's less of a machine, more interested in the people around him. That can hardly be seen as a negative." A glimmer of light filtered into Graham's mind. Maybe the same was true of him. He was also starting to see people. Starting to see nature.

"This rundown ranch was a ridiculous purchase, made only out of guilt."

"Made out of a desire to know his daughter and grandsons."

"Guilt, like I said."

When had Dad gotten this way? Graham had never seen this side of him before. Or maybe he had, and it had simply seemed as ordinary as the Italian marble or the Swedish wallpaper throughout his parents' home.

"I, for one, hope Nadine's mother agrees to meet with him."

Dad snorted. "They're only after money, the whole lot of them. That's all."

"No." Although that had certainly been Graham's thought a few months ago. Now, while he was pretty sure the Klines wouldn't turn down cash, he'd come to understand that what they wanted most was a sense of family, a sense of belonging. Didn't look like Dad would ever open up enough to offer that.

Dad shook his head. "It's worse than I thought. I'll speak to my father myself about recalling you to Chicago."

"No." When had Graham used that word so often with his dad? Never. "I'm committed to seeing this project through, however long it takes. It's been a pleasant change of pace." To his surprise, it was even true.

"One thing you need to do for sure is back off of Cadence Foster." Dad leaned in. "It's no good, you interfering in the situation with your Aunt Frances and Uncle Donald. With Paul."

"Paul is an imbecile."

The man winced. "He is your mother's sister's only son. Your only maternal cousin."

"I said what I said."

"So did I. Back off with his fiancée."

"They're not engaged anymore. Paul is the one who broke it off." And Cadence would have married the jerk if Paul hadn't gotten cold feet. Graham didn't want to think about that.

"That's not how I heard the story."

"I was there."

Dad fisted both hands as though restraining himself. "Graham. Son. Let it go. Don't let testosterone do the talking in your life."

Graham stared at his father, long and hard. "Do you love Mom?"

"But of course." Dad blinked.

"Really? Tell me what you appreciate most about her."

"She... she's strong. Independent. An attorney." Dad chuckled. Sounded a bit nervous, maybe? "She's got an answer for everything."

"So, you love her because she's always right?"

"Uh..."

Graham waited a beat, but his father didn't continue. "When I marry someone, it will be because I love her. Not because of her career or what she can bring to the family finances. Not because she's good at arguing in a court of law. But because she's kind and sweet and gentle. Because we have things in common and enjoy spending time together. Because she loves God and loves me—"

"Admirable," Dad cut in. "Just don't think that's Cadence Foster. She's taken."

"She's not property. No one owns the rights to her."

Dad made a strangled sound, pivoted on his heel, and strode away.

Graham watched him go. Had this scenario happened before, that his father hadn't been able to win an argument with him and stalked off in frustration? It wasn't the outcome Graham preferred. What would it be like to have a dad who understood him and had his back?

Cadence didn't have that, either. Her parents were as focused on renewing their relationship with the Bradleys as the other way around.

Obviously, Aunt Frances and Mom had had a heart-to-heart. Was Graham seen as that much of a threat to their desired outcome?

He wished he had as much confidence.

A SLIVER of light below the door showed someone was still in the office. Cadence stood in the corridor, hands clammy, wishing she knew who it was. She'd die of embarrassment if it were Tate, but he kept quite rigorous office hours since his marriage to Stephanie. And she'd seen Graham out on the lodge deck with his father a while ago, both of them rigid and stubborn looking. But he could have come in the other door since then. It would be like him to do so after a difficult conversation.

Why didn't she want to talk to Graham? She'd kissed him — he'd kissed her back — just… yesterday? The day before? She could barely remember. Everything had been so volatile since her parents and Paul had showed up.

She took a deep breath, tapped in the lock-code, and eased the door open.

The old man was the only one in the office, and he looked up to meet her gaze. "Cadence?"

"Um, hi, Mr. Sullivan."

He glanced over at her cubicle. "Did you forget something?"

"No, sir. I… was hoping to talk to you."

"To me?" He leaned back in his chair, surprise evident on his face. "Have a seat."

Cadence wheeled her chair near to his, perched on the edge, and tightened her hands together. "I have a problem."

"So, I've heard."

She didn't dare glance at him for fear the amusement she might have heard in his voice was real. Was he mocking her? He wouldn't do that. Hopefully.

Cadence tossed a quick prayer for wisdom and bravery heavenward. "My parents incurred quite a lot of debt planning my wedding to Paul Bradley. My mother, especially, took the reins and wanted a lavish affair."

She peeked up to see her employer's nod.

"Honestly, it was more than I wanted, but I'm their only child, only daughter, so I let her run with it. I didn't realize…" Man, she couldn't do this.

"Realize what?" Mr. Sullivan asked quietly.

She closed her eyes for a brief moment. "I think... I think my mother has a gambling problem. Or maybe it's my dad. Or maybe I've guessed wrong completely. But I think they needed this wedding to reestablish their financial foundation. Somehow, the Bradleys could fix this problem, and without the wedding, my parents stand to lose everything."

It sounded so cold and brash laid out like that. What must Mr. Sullivan think of her? Of her parents? Worse, what if she was wrong, and she'd blackballed them to a man of this esteem?

"I've heard rumors," he said, at last.

Cadence's hands dropped away from her face as she looked at him. "You have?" And... why hadn't she had a clue?

The old man's gaze was shrewd as he studied her, like he could see right into her soul. Well, she had nothing to hide.

"I don't give credence to most of what I hear. There are gossipers everywhere, most of whom only wish to make themselves look better."

"That's... true." She'd noticed it herself, a time or two.

"I doubt you are here exposing your parents in hopes I will see you in a better light than I see them."

"No, sir." She dropped her gaze and twisted her fingers tightly in her lap.

"Then why?"

"They spent money they didn't have on a wedding I ran away from."

Mr. Sullivan's chair creaked as he leaned back and

clasped his hands behind his head. "I understand Paul Bradley is the one who canceled the event."

"Yes, but… I feel responsible. Because he's asked for forgiveness, for reinstatement, and I've refused it. Doesn't that make it my problem?"

"No."

Cadence's gaze flew to the old man. "No?"

"I can understand how you feel, but two mistakes don't make things right."

"Two negatives make a positive in Math."

He dipped his head in acknowledgment. "It also works in English grammar, albeit poorly. After all, when we say something like, 'I don't *not* want to do it,' it doesn't exactly mean that you *do* want to do it. It means you'll do it, but under duress."

Like if she married Paul now. But no. She definitely did not want to, and no double negative could make it sound palatable.

"Sir? What do I do?"

Mr. Sullivan studied her as he steepled his hands in front of him. "What are your options?"

"Marry Paul."

He snorted. "Next?"

"Refuse to marry him, and let my parents lose their home."

He waited, eyebrows angled into his white hair.

Cadence took a deep breath and let the words out with a rush. "Or try to raise some money to pay my parents back for the wedding that never was. Maybe that way we'd retain some kind of relationship."

"That's very noble of you."

"I don't feel noble." If she twisted her fingers any tighter, she'd never get them untwined. "I feel... guilty."

"If one of your parents has been gambling..." He held up a finger when she startled. "I said if."

"Then what?"

"Then how do you know the money you would give them would go to repay their wedding-incurred debt and not become fuel for more speculative behavior?"

Cadence stared at her boss. "I hadn't thought of that."

"I'm not saying that would happen. We are in hypothesizing mode at the moment. If this, then possibly that."

She blew out a breath. "Right."

Mr. Sullivan leaned forward with his elbows on his desk. "You are a Christian. Are you asking for God's wisdom?"

"Yes?" Cadence hated how that came out a question. "I'm so confused. Mom and Dad are pushing me hard, and I also know that God wants us to honor our parents. How could I live with myself, if I stubbornly refuse, and they lose everything?"

"That is a dilemma."

Hope sank with barely a bubble to reveal it had ever existed. "None of the options solves anything."

"On the contrary."

"What do you mean?"

"Romans 8:28 says, 'and we know that for those who love God all things work together for good, for those who are called according to his purpose.'"

It was hard to see any positive outcome, but would the Bible lie? Maybe the Apostle Paul — or whomever had written the epistle to the Romans — hadn't understood.

Uh, now she was questioning the fallibility of scripture? She either had to believe the Bible was true... or not. And if it was, so was Romans 8:28. Was she called according to God's purpose?

Mr. Sullivan thumbed open his phone. "There's more. Listen." He skewered Cadence with a look before looking down to read. "What then shall we say to these things? If God is for us, who can be against us? He who did not spare his own Son but gave him up for us all, how will he not also with him graciously give us all things? Who shall bring any charge against God's elect? It is God who justifies."

Cadence absorbed the words. She'd have to go back and reread them for herself later.

"Who is to condemn? Christ Jesus is the one who died — more than that, who was raised — who is at the right hand of God, who indeed is interceding for us. Who shall separate us from the love of God? Shall tribulation, or distress, or persecution, or famine, or nakedness, or danger, or sword?" He paused a moment, scanning the text. "No, in all these things we are more than conquerors through him who loved us. For I am sure that neither death nor life, nor angels nor rulers, nor things present nor things to come, nor powers, nor height not depth, nor anything else in all creation, will be able to separate us from the love of God in Christ Jesus our Lord."

Mr. Sullivan set his phone down on his desk and looked at her. "What's missing?"

She gave a shaky laugh. "Not much."

"Anything at all?"

Cadence thought through the words she'd once memorized. "No. Nothing."

"Pray. Trust God to give you the wisdom you need and the courage to see it through."

"But what? What is that?"

"I'm not God. I can't answer that. But I will pray with you."

Sounded like the best she was going to get.

CHAPTER FIFTEEN

G raham hadn't ever spent this much time sitting out on the postage-stamp-sized porch to his duplex as he had in the past few days.

He'd messed up everything, and he could only think of one way to make it all right. Yeah, his solution would annoy some people — most everyone in his parents' generation — but it made sense.

Right?

Yes.

Had he prayed about it?

Also, yes. Sort of. He'd told God his idea and there had been no bolt of lightning warning him away. So, it must be good.

He took in a deep breath and let it out slowly.

It was probably a beautiful evening. A few puffy clouds scuttled across the darkening sky. A murmur of voices came from a nearby duplex, not loud enough to keep him from hearing the loons call back and forth on the little lake.

He should relax and enjoy the quiet.

But he couldn't. Not until he'd talked to Cadence. For all she'd agreed they needed to talk, she'd been mighty hard to pin down. The ranch's social media accounts proved she led a frenzied life.

The quiet hum of a golf cart alerted him to someone turning down Hummingbird Lane. Cadence. His pulse quickened as he shot to his feet and jogged into the cart's path. "Hey."

Eyes wide, she veered around him toward the quarters she shared with Paisley.

But he wasn't going to let her get away. Not this time. Graham was right there when she turned the key to the off position. "Cadence?"

His heart seized when he saw the dampness on her cheeks in the glow of the porch light. "Oh, honey. What happened?"

She stared at him, not moving off the seat. "My parents happened. Paul happened."

Yeah, he knew that. "I have—"

"They're headed back to Chicago in the morning."

Hope bubbled up. "That's good. Right?"

Cadence shook her head. "I don't know. I've only got a few more days to figure out what to do."

Graham sucked in air. "About that. I have an idea."

"You do?"

Shouldn't she sound more hopeful? He held out his hand. "Come walk with me."

Her gaze shifted to the duplex then back to him. "I'm exhausted."

It wasn't his imagination. She truly was avoiding

him... the same as he'd avoided her for an entire week. He'd been dumb. Nervous, afraid, skittish... but dumb. He couldn't let her make the same mistake. "Just for a few minutes."

"Okay." She clambered down and wrapped her arms around her middle.

Graham tugged one hand free and pulled her to walking beside him, back up the lane she'd just come down. It was darker there than toward the lake, but they wouldn't be long. Most of the creatures he feared wouldn't be prowling after dark. Except maybe mountain lions or skunks. He tightened his grip on her hand.

Now, how to begin? He racked his brain for the perfect opening, but there wasn't one.

"What did you want, Graham?"

He glanced at her profile in the dim light. Man, she was beautiful. And, yes, she looked utterly exhausted. He turned to face her, gathering both her hands in his. "Will you marry me?"

Cadence yanked her hands away and stepped back. "What?"

So much for blurting out his question. "I want to marry you. I want to love you like you deserve to be loved. I want to take care of you."

"You mean, rescue me."

He relaxed infinitesimally. She understood. "Partly that, sure. But mostly—"

"No."

Graham reared back. "But I love you."

"Do you?"

How could she even doubt him? Just because he'd kept

his feelings locked away for years didn't mean he didn't have any. Didn't meant they weren't real. "Of course, I do."

"Graham…"

This wasn't how he thought this would go down. A few days ago, it had been her coming to him, kissing him. How could she be retreating now? "What is it, sweetheart?"

"I'm not sure you love me. You hardly know me. It's… admirable that you want to step in and take care of things, but I can't let you."

"But—"

"No. You've been attracted to me for years, from what you've said. But I…" Her tone softened. "I didn't really know you, not until the past few weeks. You didn't know me, either."

That was all the time it had taken for Tate to propose to his wife, and if Stephanie had rejected Tate's proposal at first, no one had mentioned it. They hadn't even known each other way back in college. How could this be going so very wrong?

"Cadence, I love you. Please let me take care of you."

She stiffened.

Man, he'd said it wrong again. Open mouth; insert foot. But he meant it! He did. Why couldn't she see past his bumbling ways and into his heart? Because in the core of his being, all he wanted was her. Yes, to protect her, but it went way deeper.

"I'm honored, Graham. I like you. A lot. But I can't do a relationship right now. I have to figure my way through this mess, and I don't know how long that will take."

His gut iced over. Was she leaving him any hope? He wanted to protest, to remind her she'd come to him, that she'd wanted a relationship mere days ago. How had her parents and Paul messed with her so badly in so short a time? Maybe when they returned home, she'd be back to herself.

Graham studied her.

She stood partially facing away, arms tight around her middle, as she stared down the lane toward the lake, moisture glistening on her cheeks.

"Cadence," he said softly, taking a step closer.

"I can't, Graham. You'll thank me later." And she took off at a run. A moment later, the door to the home she shared with Paisley thudded shut.

Like the door to Graham's heart.

How could this be? She was hauling around a burden too heavy for her, one she didn't need to carry at all. It had been tied there by her parents, by Graham's moron cousin and his parents, but it wasn't hers.

He wanted to remove it, see her free and happy as she'd been the first few weeks she'd been at the ranch. He wanted to hear her laugh. He wanted to be with her, even if that meant sitting in a tippy kayak or atop a powerful horse. He just wanted... her.

God? Wasn't it You who put this plan in my head?

Still no booming voice from heaven, of course. Still not even a faint whisper. The only sound he heard was the crackle of a branch in the forest beside Hummingbird Lane.

And Graham wasn't sticking around long enough to figure out which of the creatures he feared was stalking him.

PAISLEY'S HEAD jerked up and her eyes widened when Cadence burst through the door. "What happened now?"

Right, because it was always something with her. She could be the star of a soap opera or a fake reality TV show with all the drama in her life.

Drama she'd brought on herself, but still.

No one pounded on the door she'd slammed shut, which meant Graham hadn't followed her. Which meant she was right, that he didn't love her, like she'd suspected.

Was there a fault in that reasoning? Possibly, but she was flailing too deeply in the whole mess to figure it out tonight.

"My parents are leaving in the morning. As is Paul."

Paisley beamed. "Excellent."

"They haven't given up."

"Then... why?"

"I think Mr. Sullivan canceled their reservation." She let out a long, slow breath. "So that gave me the nerve to go talk to him."

"The big boss."

"Yes." She'd been unbelievably stupid to do that. "I'm not sure what I expected."

"Did you ask him for a loan?"

Cadence shook her head. She'd been tempted, but maybe she'd hoped he would offer. Wouldn't she have turned him down, though? She'd turned Graham down, but that hadn't been for a loan. It had been for *marriage*.

It was super tempting. He was such a good guy. He'd never treat her as abominably as Paul had. But how could he say he loved her? He didn't know her well enough. She certainly didn't know him well enough to commit. She'd thought she'd known Paul, and she hadn't. Not even a little bit, and they'd dated for years.

"You're lost in your head," Paisley observed.

"Sorry. I don't know what to do."

"Graham was looking for you earlier."

Cadence's gut sank. "He found me. We talked outside a minute ago."

Paisley's eyebrows shot up. "Right before you sprinted in the door like the devil himself was chasing you."

Way too accurate. Cadence nodded, closing her eyes.

"What did he want?" her roommate asked quietly.

"He asked me to marry him."

Paisley hooted.

Cadence cringed. "I said no."

"You *what*? Are you insane, girl? That guy is crazy about you, plus he's absolutely loaded! He could solve all your problems with the snap of his fingers."

"Don't you see? That's exactly the issue."

"I'm lost." Paisley sprang up and patted the back of the chair next to hers. "Let me make us each a cup of tea, and you explain it to me."

"I'm beat. I need to go to bed." And not wake up for a month, when this was all over. If it ever was.

"Sit. You will drink tea." She pivoted and poured water into the kettle.

Paisley was so bossy, but Cadence was all done fighting. She sank into the chair.

"What did Mr. Sullivan say?"

Cadence rubbed her temples, trying to remember. The

encounter with Graham had driven the earlier conversation into the dim recesses of her mind. "He told me two wrongs don't make a right."

"Uh huh." Paisley eyed her. "Meaning which two wrongs?"

Good question. "I think he meant giving in to Paul a second time."

"You're not seriously considering marrying that narcissistic jerk now that you know what he's like behind the veneer."

"No. I don't think..." Man, that headache was like a band around her skull, threatening to cut off circulation. "But it's complicated."

"It's not *that* complicated. He broke up with you. You're not obligated to take him back, even if it lets your parents save face. Parents who love their kids would never ask them to take the hit that way."

"I know."

"Then why? This is a serious question."

It hadn't seemed right to dump the whole sordid mess on her roommate. Wasn't it gossip to do that? "There's more to it, but I can't get into it." She had with Mr. Sullivan, though. Why was that different? Somehow it was.

Paisley poured boiling water into her teapot, swirled it, and dumped it out before refilling it and dropping in two teabags. Something black, strong, and caffeinated, no doubt. Cadence should have refused.

Wasn't this the story of her life? All she did was cave under pressure and let other people dictate how she lived. She'd thought she was making her own decisions since college, but probably Paul and her parents had been steering her all along. The job at Lake Effect had seemed a godsend, but wasn't Mr. Harraldsson a friend of her mom's brother? Nepotism there, too. Always.

It was who you knew, not what you knew.

Even here. If Graham hadn't been the one to deliver Paul's news, she wouldn't be in Montana. He'd offered her everything she'd asked for: a job, a place to live, a refuge.

A refuge until Paul had followed her, flanked by her parents in their relentless pressure for her to marry him after all.

She owed everything to Graham, and that was why she had to put on the brakes before she went even deeper in debt to him.

Sure, he said he loved her, but how long would that profession last if he were stuck with her, day in and day out? She didn't want a marriage that was merely an escape hatch.

Cadence could come to love Graham — she was more than halfway there — but how would she know when or if her feelings were real? True? Deep?

And would his stick? His parents were too much like Paul's and her own, all consumed by what society thought of them. Staying together because showing a united front made them feel stronger, not because they loved each other. It was simply more profitable to stay put for various reasons than separate.

She didn't want a marriage like that, but it was the only model she had. The only model Graham had had. His aunt and uncle had split up, so they didn't demonstrate the kind of marriage she hoped to have one day, either.

Was true, lasting love only a fairy tale?

"Here." Paisley parked a cup of black tea on the table in front of her. "You've said you have two options, but there must be more."

"Marry Paul, or don't marry him. That's two."

"So, let's pick 'don't marry him.' What are the options then? Marry Graham — girl, I can't believe he asked you, and you turned him down!"

Cadence stared into the cup and inhaled the fragrance of bergamot as though she could draw physical strength from it. "Don't you see? I'm only a means to an end with everyone. I think... I think I just didn't run far enough away." Although Montana had seemed extremely distant from Chicago throughout the very long drive.

Paisley shook her head. "You don't have to do everything yourself. For instance — and I shouldn't have to remind you of this — there's God. He's got your best in mind. He'll lead you if you lean on Him."

"Romans 8:28. That's what Mr. Sullivan said."

"Right. Good on him." Paisley took a deep sip and let out a long, contented sigh. "There's nothing like tea to align brain cells."

Maybe it wasn't tea. Maybe it was the reminder of God. Cadence pushed back from the table. "The next verses talk about nothing separating us from the love of God."

"Right. Neither life, nor death, nor... a whole bunch of things. A pretty all-encompassing list, as I recall."

Cadence rose to her feet. "Paisley, I appreciate you, but I can't drink this tonight. Not without staying up for hours, which I might do anyway, because I have a lot to think about. But maybe I'll start with that chapter of Romans."

Paisley cradled her teacup between her palms and nodded. "I'll pray for you."

"Please do. I need all the help I can get." Cadence turned to the ladder for the loft but paused with her foot on the bottom rung. What had she just said? That she needed help. Then why couldn't she accept Graham's offer? He was never going to throw his weight around and bully her.

No, she'd made the right choice turning him down. He was a rescuer through and through, and he was responding in a way that aligned with his nature. She didn't want to be rescued. She wanted to be loved.

And hopefully the answer was in scripture.

CHAPTER SIXTEEN

A week had gone by. Sweet River Ranch was mercifully free of the Fosters and Paul Bradley, but it was a small consolation to Graham when Cadence still avoided him as though he had the plague.

If he was in the office, she wasn't. Evidence proved she'd been through from time to time. Social media pages were updated, and new photos of the ranch's landscape sprouted up on the website.

"You're going to Harper and Eli's wedding tomorrow, right? I saw your name on the list of who's going from up here."

Graham turned to study his cousin Tate. "I'm reconsidering. I'm not much in the mood for weddings, and I don't know either of them all that well."

Eli Bryson was the youth pastor at Creekside Fellowship in town, and he was marrying Tate's wife's previous roommate. Also, hadn't Stephanie once dated Eli? The whole thing sounded awkward from the get-go.

"Aw, you should go anyway and get to know some of

the townsfolk. Besides, everyone deserves a day off, and we've got everything covered across the ranch already. What would you do if you stayed back? Read a book?"

Graham glowered at Tate. "Maybe? I'm in the midst of a thriller trilogy."

"If I thought you'd take a horse or a kayak out, I might leave you be, but not if you're going to mope."

"I'm not moping."

Tate studied him.

Graham narrowed his gaze and stared back.

"Uh, yeah, I think that's what you've been doing ever since your other cousin, the dumbhead, showed up along with Cadence's parents. Don't let them take all the wind out of your sails."

"I have no sails," he replied stiffly.

"Obviously. But you did there for a while. The smiling Graham was fun to be around."

"Sorry for not meeting your expectations."

"Now you're sounding as grumpy as Weston."

"Stuff it."

"You know what, Graham? You're a good guy. I honestly never knew that before the past few months, so I'm thankful for Grandfather pushing us here for that, at least."

"To say nothing of Stephanie."

A wide grin creased Tate's face and lit his eyes. "Well, she's not part of the equation between you and me, but you're right. She's made all the difference in many ways."

Graham turned away. He wanted what Tate had, only with Cadence. And minus the toddler. The joy and contentment on his cousin's face jabbed deep into his own discomfort and twisted. Why had Cadence turned him down? Why didn't she see that he loved her and would help her solve the problems that had overtaken her? He could extricate her from any financial difficulties she found herself in. He'd do anything for her.

"We'll be staying late. Stephanie is Harper's matron-of-honor, so her parents are keeping Jamie overnight, but you could get a ride down with Bryce and Maxwell if you didn't want to drive down yourself."

The Creekside Fellowship parking lot was sure to be jammed. Everyone in Jewel Lake would be present to see the youth pastor tie the knot, and Harper came from enough money that the size of the wedding was no issue.

Graham preferred the Sundays Eli preached over Pastor Marshall Smith, truth be told. The younger man had a way of presenting God's truth that resonated with him. Like all the teaching on treasure during the church's annual Pot of Gold Geocaching Hunt over the summer.

Pastor Smith would be handling the wedding, and the man had been married for probably forty years. He might have some insights Graham could use.

If Graham ever married.

If Cadence would have him someday.

Someone else? His innermost being rejected that question. Cadence was it for him after all they'd shared in the past six weeks. Look at his history since college. Whenever he'd thought to ask a girl out, he'd compared her to Cadence, and any allure had dissipated. And that was before they'd reconnected. Before she noticed him at all.

He was a fool to have moved slowly at first, thinking she needed time to get over Paul. And he was a fool to have jumped straight to a proposal last week. See? He was socially inept.

Cadence was better off without him.

If only he could convince himself of that, when every molecule in his body yearned to smooth the way in front of her.

"—looking forward to listening to the wedding sermon," Tate said.

"Huh?" Graham wished he could bite back the interjection. "Sorry, I wasn't listening."

"I could tell. What I said was, the last time I heard a good sermon on marriage was at Wally and Ashley's wedding. I didn't pay much attention. Too busy doing all the best man stuff, I guess."

Graham had attended Tate's older brother's wedding as well. He didn't have the same excuse for not remembering the details.

"And then Eli preached a doozy at Stephanie's and my wedding." Tate grinned. "I've listened to it a couple of times since from the recording. Either way, I'm looking forward to Pastor Smith's take on the subject. Seems like a man always has a lot to learn about how to love a woman. It doesn't come naturally to us."

Graham blinked. "You make it look so easy."

Tate threw his head back and guffawed. "Oh, I wish."

"But…"

Tate shook his head, though the smile remained. "We didn't know each other all that well."

"True." At least Graham had known Cadence for years. Except… had he really? They hadn't even hung out, let alone dated.

"We had some stuff to work through, and I'm sure there will be more." Tate let out a breath. "I want to be up for each and every challenge. I don't want there to be any space between us for problems to fester, you know? Like what broke my parents' marriage apart."

"You put your foot down hard about office hours with Grandfather."

"I did." Tate smirked. "Which was a good first step, but there's more, every day. Stephanie is complicated. But I bet she's no more complicated than other women."

Graham tried to wrap his head around what Tate was saying. "Do you wish you hadn't married her?" If that were true, he didn't want to know it.

"Not at all. I love her like crazy. I'm only saying it's not a walk in the park, but it's worth every single minute. And that I hope Pastor Smith has some good relationship tips I can take home from that wedding sermon. Maybe you'll find some, too."

What did his cousin think he knew? Everything was probably written all over Graham's face, and it wouldn't take much genius to have noticed that he and Cadence had spent a lot of time together in the first few weeks but that things had gotten increasingly awkward ever since.

Tate didn't need to know about Graham's botched proposal to realize there was trouble in paradise.

Had there ever been paradise?

For a few brief weeks, Graham had thought it might be a possibility. He glanced at his cousin. "Maybe so."

"I'M COMING, TOO."

Cadence glanced toward the stable's corridor to see Weston standing with his arms crossed and his cowboy hat tugged low.

"We've got it!" Paisley yelled from the next box stall over. "We don't need a chaperone."

Cadence cringed at the volume as she soothed Mirage's restless wince.

"Ranger needs exercise, too."

"Ride him some other direction."

"No."

Cadence sighed. Had she been looking forward to her roommate's snoopy, pointed questions? Not really. Problem was, she doubted Paisley would be deterred by Weston's presence. That girl had no filter.

Aside from the Sullivans, the Klines, and a few others who'd been at a wedding in town, everyone had pitched in yesterday to make operations run smoothly for their full house of guests. Even Maxwell's construction crew had hung around and set up an obstacle course for the kids on the main lawn by the lodge, something Paisley would usually have done.

Was Paisley acquainted with the bride and groom? Not that Cadence knew of, but she'd gone to the wedding. No one was a stranger to Paisley Teele. Not for long, anyway.

It had made for the most relaxing day Cadence had experienced yet at Sweet River. Graham and Paisley had both been absent. Her luck had run out today at her roommate's insistence on a horseback ride.

Now all she needed was Weston, too. The guy perpetually seemed mildly amused by something, which should have gone against his surly persona, but somehow didn't. He must think he was a cut above the rest of creation to look down on them like that.

Weston's horse nickered, and Cadence could hear his quiet voice soothe the gelding. She'd only ever heard him use that tone with horses. Might do him some good to try it on people, not that she'd be fooled for one red hot second.

"Ready?" Paisley stood outside Mirage's stall, holding Enchantment's lead.

"Yep." Cadence checked the cinch one final time, led her mare into the corridor, then followed Paisley and Enchantment out into the bright sunshine. She swung up on Mirage's back as Paisley mounted her horse. "Where to?"

"The trail along the Sweet River," Paisley said quietly with a glance to the stable door.

"Good choice." Weston came through and vaulted onto Ranger's back. "After you."

What on earth was going on between the two of them? Cadence wasn't sure she wanted to know, but the awkwardness was thick like wildfire smoke and stank as badly. She didn't wish that kind of confusion on anyone, not after the spring and summer she'd endured.

In a mere few weeks, her commitment to Sweet River would be done. What would she do then? Certainly not hang around and watch Graham try to move on. Also, no going back to Chicago. She needed to start scrounging for a job somewhere else. Something that paid well so that she could continue sending money to her parents. Not that she'd received any thanks for the check she'd sent, although it had been cashed.

Paisley led the way up the trail, and Cadence nudged Mirage into step behind the duo. She could hear Weston on Ranger behind her.

Awkward. And since her roommate seemed to be in a huff, she'd talk to the cowboy. She angled her head to speak behind her. "How was the wedding yesterday?"

"All right, as leg-shacklings go."

Guys. Weddings. Maybe that was the best she could expect. But she could try a little harder. "Lots of people?"

"Yeah. Harper's family is loaded." Silence a moment. "Sort of like the Sullivans, I guess."

She didn't want to talk about the Sullivans. "You're one of them."

He snorted. "Shirt-tail relative from the wrong side of the tracks that no one wants to acknowledge."

Cadence frowned. "Your grandfather gave you a job, same as your cousins." Unless he didn't pay Weston and Jude as much? That didn't make sense, though.

"Jobs suited for country hicks."

She angled in her saddle to see the cowboy more clearly. "I thought you loved horses."

"Sure."

Then what was his problem? She bit the impatient question off before she could voice it. It was none of her business. She'd be gone from Sweet River Ranch in a few short weeks, and then she'd never have to wonder again if Weston and his brother had ever found themselves in the bosom of the Sullivan family.

Right, she could tell herself that all she wanted, but Graham and his clan wouldn't disappear out of her thoughts with a wipe of the slate.

"That ex of yours is a nutjob."

And Weston wasn't telling her something she didn't already know. "He is."

"He tried to talk me into letting him take a horse out several times while he was here."

Cadence frowned. Paul rode? She'd never known that about him in all the years they'd dated. She couldn't imagine him on horseback, but maybe? He was fairly athletic, at least compared to his cousin.

And there, her thoughts had circled back to Graham, just like she'd promised herself they wouldn't. She'd be on guard. Right, nice try.

She glanced back at Weston. "Did he ride?"

"No. He wanted Ranger, and there's no way I'm letting a screwball city slicker ride my horse. He also wanted to know which one you usually rode."

Cadence's heart stumbled. "Did you tell him?" He wouldn't hurt Mirage, would he?

Weston snorted. "Are you kidding? I didn't trust that dude as far as I could throw him. Every question he asked, I evaded or lied when I answered."

"Thanks." Maybe. But what had Weston seen so instantly in Paul to cause such a strong reaction?

"Anything for a friend."

Unexpected. Moisture in her eyes blurred the trail ahead. Would she have considered Weston Kline a friend of hers? He wouldn't have made her short list, that's for sure.

She swiped the dampness away, only then becoming aware that Paisley was no longer in sight. "Why is Paisley mad at you?"

Weston harrumphed. "She's a stick of dynamite, that one. Always poking her nose where it doesn't belong."

Cadence could attest to that.

"Just gave her a piece of her own medicine, that's all."

And there was a story Cadence would need to get to the bottom of.

CHAPTER SEVENTEEN

Grandfather cleared his throat. "I contacted Eleanor."

Graham pivoted in his desk chair and stared at the old man. Neither Tate nor Cadence was in the office this late in the day — not that Cadence hardly ever came in since the day he'd proposed. "You what?"

"You heard me, boy."

Yeah, he had, but that didn't mean he believed his ears. "Are you meeting up with her?"

"That's up to her."

How much harder could Grandfather make this moment? "Tell me what happened."

"We had a bargain, you and me."

Graham's heart sank. "We did."

"So, if I spill my guts, so will you."

It wasn't a question or a request. But it wasn't like Graham had followed through. He had, but he'd made a total flop of the whole thing. "Yes, sir. You first."

A glimmer of amusement shone from the old man's eyes. "Don't think I won't hold you to that."

"I know."

Grandfather let out a long breath. "I asked Nadine for her mother's contact information. It took her the better part of a week to give it to me."

"She had to check with Eleanor, first," Graham guessed.

"Right. Which makes sense, but the delay made me crazy. Once I'd decided to move forward, I wanted to go full-bore."

Graham had never felt more understanding for his grandfather than at that moment. Wasn't that what had gone wrong with Cadence? His own impatience? And the fact that he'd leaped over what should have been weeks' more of talking and getting to know each other.

He was lousy at small talk. He lived for the moment when both columns of numbers matched, not for a bunch of if-then statements. Was Walter Sullivan like that, too? Maybe they were more alike than he'd ever considered.

"What happened after that?" he asked cautiously.

"Eleanor lives in Missoula now. With her son, Nadine's half-brother."

"That's not far away at all."

"It's not. I thought she was up near Kalispell, which, in the grand scheme of things, isn't far, either."

Graham nodded. Waited.

"But now that I have a street address, I find myself wanting to drive into town and watching for a glimpse of her."

"But you're waiting on her to invite you. Right?"

"It's an older house. Shabby."

"You looked it up on street view?" Graham shouldn't be surprised. He'd have done the same thing, and Grandfather was at least as astute with technology as he was.

"Of course." Grandfather shrugged and looked down at his phone. "Want to see?"

"Why not?" Graham accepted the device and studied the older house. It wasn't huge, but it wasn't tiny, either. The siding and white picket fence might be in need of a paint job, but the yard overflowed with roses. "Someone loves flowers." He handed the phone back.

"She always had a bouquet on her desk." Grandfather stared into the image. "I teased her about her boyfriend, but she said she bought them for herself since they brightened her life." He huffed out a breath as he shook his head. "Why did I take advantage of her? She didn't deserve to think she'd lose her job if she didn't give in to me."

"Did you... force her?" Graham couldn't believe he had enough nerve to ask that question, but after what his grandfather had said...

"No. But, if memory serves, I probably came close to that line. Times were different, boy." Grandfather pursed his lips. "But not that different. I regret my actions a great deal."

"You've been in contact, you said. Did you tell her you were sorry?"

"I did."

"And her response?"

Grandfather swallowed hard. "She forgave me a long time ago, she said. Water under the bridge and all that. And she loves Nadine and could hardly wish her not born. I only wish... no. It was better this way."

When the old man didn't seem ready to go on, Graham nudged. "You only wish what?"

"I wish she'd told me why she left Chicago. I'd have done the right thing. I'd have married her, taken care of her and our daughter."

"But then..." Graham waved around the place then pointed at himself.

"I know. Your grandmother and I were happy together. I loved her. I did, even though I made her crazy and failed her often. I love your father and your uncle. All you boys."

Graham wasn't sure he'd ever heard Grandfather voice the L word before, let alone more than once in one conversation. Let alone referring to him.

"You know that Robert Frost poem, "The Road Not Taken"?"

"Uh... yes?" At least, Graham had a vague memory of studying it back in school. "Something about a crossroads, and the poet took the path less traveled by."

"*And that has made all the difference,*" Grandfather quoted, musing. "The point being, I suppose, that for every path we select, we are choosing not to explore all the other ones."

Who knew the old man had such a philosophical bent? Graham had never suspected it. And yet, did it take poetry to make a man realize he couldn't test every fork in the road before committing? Wasn't that simple common sense? He shook his head. Give him mathematical equations any day of the week.

"So, we've exchanged a couple of emails, and she waits several days before responding." Grandfather harrumphed. "Has she forgotten I'm eighty years old? If she keeps that up, I'll die of old age before we finish the conversation."

Graham couldn't help the chuckle.

Thankfully, his grandfather joined with a self-deprecating cough before pinning his eagle eyes on him. "Now, you."

Oh, boy. Graham took a long breath. "I asked Cadence to marry me, and she turned me down."

Grandfather blinked and leaned back in his chair, studying him before shaking his head. "You… what?"

"The answer to all the problems is so simple. If she married me, her parents and Paul would have to back off. I could easily negotiate the canceled wedding payments and—"

"Pardon me." Grandfather waved a hand. "You pitched marriage like a business deal?"

Graham closed his eyes and gathered what little remained of his courage. "Too much so, I think." And wasn't that just what Paul had done? Graham was such a moron.

"Do you love her?"

What was with all this love-talk all of a sudden? "Of course, I do. What's not to love? She's amazing. Beautiful. Kind."

Grandfather muttered something Graham couldn't quite catch.

"What?"

"Even in my day, a man had to be more romantic than that to get his girl. You have to woo her, boy. You could say those things about nearly any woman. About Stephanie. About Paisley. About Kaci, or Heather, or—"

"Stop." Graham held up his hand. "Stephanie's married. The others are nice enough, but I don't love any of them. Only Cadence."

"Then you need more than beautiful and kind. What makes her special to you? Why her and not Kaci? Is it because you can solve her financial dilemma?"

"Of course not."

"Then why?"

Why, indeed? And did he need to get down to brass tacks like that? He thought back to Pastor Smith's homily at Eli and Harper's wedding last week. Were all wedding sermons based on First Corinthians 13? Maybe he should reread the passage and figure out what love was. How his love for Cadence was different from how he loved others.

"Did you tell her you love her?"

Graham thought back to the conversation that dark night. "I did, but maybe too little, too late."

Yeah, he needed some time in God's word before he could figure this out.

WHAT WAS LOVE?

Cadence knew the definition, sort of. She knew she wanted to be the recipient of it, not only the giver. But the more times she'd gone over Graham's ridiculously awkward proposal, the more she'd realized that he hadn't intended it the way it had come across.

Yeah, he wanted to rescue her. An admirable quality, right? But he'd also said he loved her, and she'd thrown that back in his face, told him he didn't know what love was.

Like she was some sort of expert. Ha. Obviously not, or she wouldn't have lashed out at him that way.

Graham would probably always remain a little bit awkward. He wasn't smooth and suave like Paul and most of the guys she'd been around since college. But look where that had brought her.

If she ever married, it would be for love. She'd *know* she was in love. She'd know the guy was worthy of her love and wouldn't misuse her trust.

But how could a woman know for sure? She was only human, after all, and people were good at hiding things. Of showing the side of themselves they wanted others to see.

She was guilty of that herself. Always breezy. Always smiling in the selfies she took for social media. She'd learned how to make her eyes crinkle to make that smile look absolutely genuine every time.

Was that persona what Graham thought he loved?

No. He'd seen behind the facade. He'd been there to pick up the pieces and help her escape the mess she'd made.

He'd rescued her.

And around she went. She couldn't hate him for that being part of his nature, even when she felt embarrassed that he felt the need to take care of her that way. That he saw her as weak, when she wanted to be seen as strong.

Lord, help me.

Didn't the Bible talk about true love? She tapped a search into her phone. First Corinthians 13 showed at the top of the results. She'd read that dozens of times. What else was there? Another link pointed to 1 John 4, so she opened that one and scanned the words.

Beloved, let us love one another, for love is from God, and whoever loves has been born of God and knows God. Anyone who does not love does not know God, because God is love. In this the love of God was made manifest among us, that God sent his only Son into the world, so that we might live through him. In this is love, not that we have loved God but that he loved us and sent his Son to be the propitiation for our sins. Beloved, if God so loved us, we also ought to love one another. No one has ever seen God; if we love one another, God abides in us and his love is perfected in us.

She re-read the verses. God's love was manifested in Jesus' sacrifice for her. Wasn't that a rescue? Maybe Graham wasn't as far off as she'd thought.

Could a person love someone else, someone who had needs — Cadence winced at the enormity of hers — and not even try to alleviate the burdens caused by them?

God saw the chaos people had created and loved them so much He rescued them. Or at least formed a plan to do so, but it was up to each individual to decide whether to activate that plan or not.

She'd taken that rescue for granted, but had she fully accepted it? Embraced it?

Propitiation, though. What was that all about? She looked it up. Atonement. Appeasement. Jesus met the requirements for her sins. She'd known that, of course.

Cadence stared at the creek bubbling its way out of the lake on its way to the Clark Fork. Sweet River, named for the sweetgrass plant. Didn't First Nations people revere it for its aroma that symbolized healing and peace?

Healing and peace. Wasn't that what she needed? But it wouldn't be found in a plant, aromatherapy notwithstanding. It would only be found in Jesus.

She inhaled deeply, trying to discern the vanilla-like fragrance amid the other sub-alpine blooms that crowded the creek bank and swept up into the meadow. She closed her eyes. A summer breeze flirted with her cheek and whispered in her hair. The sun's warmth filtered through the dappling of overhanging trees, aspens and conifers alike. A mountain lark sang a delicate melody in the distance, and a bee or two droned nearby.

Slowly, slowly, the tension eased out of Cadence's muscles.

God was here. He'd created this amazing place and filled it with everything needed to tantalize all her senses.

He loved her.

And yes, deliverance was part of that love.

For God so loved the world, that he gave his only Son, that whoever believes in him should not perish but have eternal life.

How had she thought love could exist without rescue? That it was somehow separate?

Graham wasn't God. Not even a little bit, but he was trying to show his love in a way that God did — by offering her a way of escape.

Why was she having such a hard time accepting it from him?

CHAPTER EIGHTEEN

Summer was dwindling to a close. Schools across the country had started fall classes, but there were still plenty of families vacationing at Sweet River Ranch. Weston and his crew still offered trail rides and horseback lessons. Paisley still offered daily programming for kids, and many of them still splashed and squealed at the lake's small beach when nothing else was on the agenda.

And where was Cadence?

If Graham didn't have access to the resort's Instagram and Facebook pages, he'd barely know she was still around. He caught a glimpse of her here and there, usually disappearing in the distance.

He didn't have time to sit in the dining hall the entire time the lines were open simply to catch sight of her. Not if she was this desperate to reject him.

He'd blown it, possibly forever. See, this was why he'd never made a move back in college. He was hopelessly incompetent, and he'd known he would mess up. Better not to even go there.

A twenty-eight-year-old Graham had done very little thinking that night in June when he'd stood up to Paul then facilitated the breakup. And then offered Cadence a job and a place to live and a ride west.

Now he stared out the office window as shadows lengthened across the lake. The mess was inevitable. It was who he was. He should have kept his mouth shut.

No, he shouldn't. He should have rescued Cadence, either way. She deserved to be happy. To be loved.

Whatever made him think he could be the one to love her?

Whoever let him open his mouth and try to rescue her a second time?

And now he was contemplating doing it a third time. He stared at the listing that hadn't even gone live yet in Chicago. The bank was about to foreclose on Cadence's parents' house.

Third time was the charm, right? No one would ever have to know it was him who bought their house. Though what could he do with it anonymously? Maybe hiding behind a business name...

Was it better to be upfront? Was it better not to make a move at all? How could he sit here, knowing he could make the difference, and not do anything? He couldn't live with himself.

Graham rubbed his hands through his hair, bumping his glasses askew. He'd spent so much time in the office lately that his eyes burned from the contact lenses. Also, there was no one to impress. No one cared.

A tap sounded and the office door opened.

Graham pivoted his chair toward it. Grandfather rarely spent the evening in here these days. Seemed Tate had convinced the old man to keep reasonable office hours.

Bryce stuck his head around. "Hey, it's you."

"Uh... yes? Who were you expecting?"

"I was hoping to talk to Grandfather."

"About?" Sheesh, now Graham sounded like the boss's secretary.

"Personal stuff." Bryce eyed him. "What are you doing here so late? A problem with the accounts the rest of us should know about?"

"No, everything's okay."

"Then, why?" Bryce waved his hand. "I thought Tate made sure things were locked down by five-thirty these days. I saw the light from outside and thought maybe Grandfather was in here. Didn't expect you."

"Well, it's me. I'm analyzing some real estate in Chicago."

Bryce's eyebrows shot up. "Buying a place and moving back so soon? I didn't know any of us had been released."

Graham leaned back in his chair. "Considering options, is all. One of these days he'll have to relent, right? I can easily do all this from back home. He doesn't need me here."

"He doesn't need me, either. Anyone could keep up the landscaping." His cousin grimaced. "Still, I hate to say it, but this place is growing on me. Max and I have been riding pretty regularly. Never thought I'd think it was fun."

Graham had ridden twice. Once with Tate and Stephanie, and once with Cadence. The day they'd acknowledged some feelings. The day he'd begun to stick his neck out and started the process of failing once again.

"You been riding?"

"Uh, not much. Not my thing."

"There are fewer bugs this time of year. Fewer reptiles." Graham tried to still his suddenly pounding heart. "You've seen snakes?"

"Yeah, a few times, up on a hot rock on a sunny day."

"You've succeeded in reminding me why I love indoors so much."

Bryce laughed. "I get it, man. But the outdoors is pretty great, too. We've learned to watch out for critters and give them a wide berth. Thankfully there aren't too many in this area."

"And then there are mountain lions and bears." Hopefully Graham had kept his trepidation out of his voice.

"We've seen a few bears, too. Blacks, Weston says, from the photos Maxwell snapped. Weston says they're more afraid of us than we are of them, and just to treat them with respect. And never come between a sow and her cubs."

"Like any mama, I guess." Except maybe his own. Graham's mother had always been too busy in the office to be a mommy. Seeing Stephanie step into that role with Jamie made Graham's heart hurt even more for the little boy he'd been himself. His own nanny had certainly never loved him like that.

Maybe it was Graham. Maybe he was unlovable.

God loved him. Right? Right. But then, why did no one else?

"Yeah," Bryce agreed.

Took Graham a minute to remember what he was talking about. Mothers. That had been the topic. "You wanting to get back to Chicago soon? Over the winter?"

"Man, I don't know. I never thought I wanted to leave Chi-Town, but after everything came apart with Madison, and we broke up, I didn't much care anymore. You know what I mean?"

No, Graham did not know. He'd never had a long-term relationship. "What happened with Madison?" There'd been some talk last spring, but he'd never quite figured it out. Not that it was any of his business, but he felt like he knew his cousins better now than he had back then.

"She wanted to get serious, and I didn't. She... went kind of weird and wouldn't leave me alone about it."

"Madison wanted to get married, and you didn't?"

Bryce sighed. "I messed up, okay? Like, really messed up. I was ignoring my faith, and we got physically involved. Then she figured she owned me and wanted me to put a ring on it. And I panicked."

Well. Graham slumped back in his chair. Had everyone had sex but him? And why did his mind even go there, like virginity was something to regret? "So, you didn't love her?"

"I don't know, man." Bryce shoved his hand through his hair in a motion very like Graham's. Did their fathers do it, too? Grandfather did.

"So, you had sex with someone you didn't love."

Bryce glared. "Why would I expect you to understand? I thought I was headed that way with Madison, but when you put the cart before the horse, so to speak, it's a little more difficult to figure out. I have regrets."

Who had last said that? Besides Graham himself, of course. Grandfather. Graham studied his cousin. "Did she get pregnant?"

Bryce shook his head. "She was on the pill. Which should have told me something right there."

No point in agreeing too heartily. It wasn't like Graham could offer any advice out of his own vast wisdom. "You never mentioned what you wanted with Grandfather this late."

"And you never told me who you're hiding from by being in the office this late."

"Hiding? I'm not hiding."

"Cadence, right?"

Was he an open book everyone could read? "She hates me."

Bryce snorted. "I doubt it. Maybe all she needs is some time."

Time was running out. Soon Cadence would find out about the pending foreclosure, if she didn't already. Was she keeping in touch with her parents? Were they still applying pressure?

How could he know the answers if she kept avoiding him?

CADENCE COULD SNAP her fingers and make everything better. She could get Paul off her back, she could save her parents' financial difficulties, she could... what? What was in it for her?

All she needed to do was tell Graham she'd marry him.

Would it be so terrible? He was a nice guy, if a little awkward. He was trying to live out his faith. Paul wasn't a nice guy, and he was definitely not trying to live like Jesus.

She should make the call and get rid of his pressure once and for all.

But Graham and Paul were cousins, so if she married Graham, she'd still wind up seeing Paul at family functions, at least occasionally. Paul wasn't that easy to be rid of.

So, her best bet was starting over even further from Chicago than Jewel Lake, Montana. This ranch had seemed like the distant ends of the earth only two months ago. Now it wasn't nearly far enough away.

California?

She couldn't see herself as a California girl, but one of her college friends lived in Sacramento and seemed to like it. Cadence should see if Judith knew of any job openings.

But she might need to buy a car if she were venturing so far. In Chicago, she'd taken the L everywhere.

And she had stuff still stored in her parents' garage, unless Mom, in a fit of pique, had gotten rid of Cadence's winter clothes and Christmas decorations and the last couple of boxes of paperbacks. Good thing she'd started reading on her tablet. And maybe in California she wouldn't need her parka or snow boots.

Why wasn't the way clear?

She couldn't drag Graham into this. He was a nice guy. He'd get over her and find someone whose life wasn't such a mess. Someone who wasn't in need of rescue but could come to him on a more equal basis.

Paisley breezed into the duplex. "Hey! I wondered where you'd gotten to."

"I thought I'd make dinner in tonight. I got Nadine to add a few supplies for me on her last order. You're welcome to join me if you like."

"Aw, you should have given me more warning! I'm here to shower after playing running games with the tweens all afternoon, and then I'm meeting Kaci and Heather in the dining hall. I thought you'd join us."

Cadence shook her head. "Nah."

"You've been missing in action a lot lately, for someone whose job is *social* media." Paisley air-quoted the words. "Doesn't that require being sociable?"

"Not feeling it today."

"Or yesterday. Want to talk about it?"

"Not really. It's stuff from back home."

"The Paul thing."

"Partly, yeah."

Paisley harrumphed. "I thought you'd told him no, go away, don't come back."

"I did, but he's nothing if not persistent."

"Has he vowed his undying love?"

"He has not." Far from it, actually. If he thought his increasingly pushy wording was going to sway her, he was more of a loser than she'd ever thought possible.

"I thought you blocked him."

"I did, but I'd have to get a new phone myself to block every number he calls from." Trust him to have access to everything he needed to keep stalking her.

"So, do it."

Cadence rubbed her thumb against her fingertips in the *it takes money* gesture. "And before you ask, my parents need my number, and they'd give it to Paul again, anyway."

"I want to say I don't understand how your parents could be such jerks, but then I think of my own mother, and I remember most of us don't have an ideal family."

"You've never mentioned your dad." Maybe she could turn the conversation away from her own issues, since there was nothing her roommate could do to solve them, anyway.

Paisley shrugged. "Never met the guy."

"Ouch."

"Yeah, well, that's my reality. I have a couple of sisters, but I doubt we have the same fathers. Mom was, well, a piece of work."

"Was?"

"She kicked her addiction about five years ago. She's trying to be a mother now, but it's too little, too late, you know? You can't get back all those years of neglect."

"I can't imagine."

Paisley managed a wan smile. "Be thankful you don't have to. Your parents, now. They've got problems, too, and it's wrong of them to drag you into them. To count on you saving them from their own lousy choices."

Was that all it was? Maybe? All Cadence knew was that the guilt was real. She had it in her hands to solve their problems two different ways, and all she was doing about it was digging in her heels while wringing her hands.

Marrying Paul was a no-go. They couldn't talk her into that, no matter what.

Marrying Graham was far more tempting, but she couldn't bring herself to agree to it. Not when she knew it was only his rescuer complex talking, because the real Graham Sullivan was much too shy to make such an offer without that knight-on-a-white-horse syndrome going on.

Which meant he didn't love her, for all he'd tacked the words onto his awkward proposal. He loved the idea of her. Of saving her.

Paisley rocked from one foot to the other. "Well, it's the shower for me. Are you sure you won't come down to the dining room with the gang?"

"You go ahead."

"I worry about you."

Cadence forced out a smile and made certain it reached her eyes. "I'm fine, really. Have fun with the girls."

"Okay. If you're sure."

"Absolutely. I'm peopled out after a busy day around the resort. I'm only here for another two weeks, so—"

"Wait. What? You're leaving?"

"I only promised to stay through Labor Day."

"Yeah, but…" Paisley shook her head. "Never mind. You do you. Just so you know Graham Sullivan is madly in love with you."

Cadence chuckled. Did it sound natural? She could hope. "I'm pretty sure you're wrong about that, but nice try."

"Where are you going? Not back to Chicago, I hope."

"Never."

"Then where? Why? I don't understand."

"I haven't given my notice yet, so don't go blabbing, you hear? Not to the big boss, but not to Kaci or Heather or the others, either."

Paisley sighed. "You drop a bombshell like that on me

and tell me to zip? You need to do a better job explaining why."

"It's time. There's no future for me here. I need to find where there is." And with whom, if not Graham. Did he truly love her and was just weird about it? Maybe. But how did a woman ask a question like that of the man she crushed on? She couldn't.

Although she was pretty sure it was more than a crush. Graham was everything she could ever want, if only he'd stop trying to rescue her from herself. Or… if only she could let him.

Or make the first move.

Hmm. Was it worth making a fool of herself to find out if Graham's interest was real and genuine and not just because she couldn't seem to manage without help?

It wasn't like she could walk up to him and ask him point-blank. He had too much honor to back down. So, if not that way, then how could she know for sure?

CHAPTER NINETEEN

Graham grabbed his laptop and headed across the great room to the conference room. Tate didn't usually schedule meetings over there, and there hadn't been one on the company calendar yesterday. Maybe Tate had baby brain and had forgotten to enter it in the agenda in advance? Ever since he and Stephanie had announced they were expecting, Tate's head had been stuck in some cloud or other.

Nice for them.

Graham winced. Even the tone of his internal thoughts had turned sour over this thing with Cadence. Why was he such a bumbling idiot?

He entered the conference room, flipped on the lights, and closed the door. Where were Tate and everyone else? He turned and blinked.

Cadence stood leaning against the window ledge. She turned toward him as he entered. "Hi."

"Hi." His voice cracked like an adolescent. But man, she was beautiful. He'd missed seeing her so much that now his eyes couldn't get enough of looking at her. "I thought Tate called a meeting?"

She shook her head. "Sorry. I needed to talk to you in private."

Like she didn't know where he lived, or that he'd give her five minutes or five hours or a lifetime if she only asked. He swallowed hard. "Okay. I'm here."

"I've been thinking about things."

So had he. He nodded and waited.

"This is super hard. You know I'm over a barrel here. My parents and Paul are still pressuring me."

"Still?" Graham's eyebrows shot up. He'd figured he'd solved that problem already, but maybe things all took a little time to wend through the systems.

"Mom called again this morning." Cadence poked her toe against a chair leg in front of her. "She came clean. Or I think she did. They're in a bad way, about to lose the house, but something weird happened, and they got an offer for it out of the blue. It wasn't even listed for sale, just in early foreclosure proceedings."

Graham's heart hammered. "What did she say about it?"

"Not much. She pleaded with me not to let it come to that. She seems to think that if I gave in to Paul, everything would turn up roses immediately." Cadence shook her head. "But that doesn't even make sense. Even if I flew to Chicago today and married him tomorrow, how would that help their financial state? Doesn't it take time?"

He needed to be extremely careful what he said here. How would she take it when she figured out what he'd done? She certainly hadn't asked him to interfere. "I would think so, unless they have an insanely good lawyer on retainer." Like Graham's mother, Paul's aunt. But Mom wouldn't do that for her greedy sister, would she? He didn't think so, but what did he know? People surprised him all the time.

Cadence turned away so only her profile was to him. "You offered another solution. You asked me to... m-marry you."

His heart forgot to beat, and his hands grew clammy. "I did. But I messed that up."

"Do you still mean it?"

"Yes, but—"

"Never mind. If there's a but, I don't want to hear it." She pivoted to the window.

Were her shoulders trembling? They were. Drat, she was crying, and he'd caused it. Everything in him wanted to cross the space, take her in his arms, and kiss her worries away.

His feet held their ground. "I need to tell you something."

"Graham, don't. Just don't. I'll figure something else out." She whirled toward the door.

He stepped in front of it, and she stopped several feet away. "You don't need to save your parents. You definitely don't need to marry Paul."

"You wouldn't make sacrifices for your parents? Of course, you'd never need to. Your parents are filthy rich. There's nothing they need from you or anyone else."

Graham winced. She wasn't far off, and therein lay part of his problem growing up. They didn't need anything from him. Didn't need an embarrassment like him at all.

"I'm sorry I got Tate to send you over here. Now, may I please leave?"

"I have more to say. And you need to hear it."

Cadence's shoulders drooped. "Get it over with. I can't imagine being more humiliated than I already am."

Graham sucked in a deep breath. Here went nothing. "That offer on your parents' house? It's me. I want to sign the deed over to you. You can let them live there if you want, or not. It's up to you. No strings attached."

"You *what?*" Her voice was tinged with hysteria, and her eyes bulged.

"I did it because I love you. I want you to be free to make your own choices." Man, this was hard. "I would love to marry you, but not because you need to escape a bad situation. If you want to say yes to me, it will be because you love me in return."

"You're undeniably, irrevocably crazy."

That was his answer, then. Graham dipped his head in acknowledgment and stepped away from the doorway. "Part of me wants to say I'll retract that offer if it makes you so frustrated, but... no. My reasons are valid. If you marry Paul, it's because you want to. If you marry me, it's because you want to. If you find some other guy, fall in love, and marry him, that's your choice. No one can force your hand, Cadence. You're free."

Since she hadn't made a move to escape the conference room, he gave her one more nod and strode from the room, his laptop still tucked under his arm. He kept an ear cocked in that direction. She'd call him back, right? Tell him she loved him. Thank him for a rescue that set her free. Kiss him and tell him she wanted to marry him with no strings attached.

But only silence came from behind him. He crossed the great room without looking to see who might be observing him, ducked into the opposite hallway, then realized Tate knew about the meeting and would be curious how it turned out. Graham didn't want to talk about it. He marched past the office door and out the far exit.

Now what? He paused under the overhang and allowed his eyes to adjust to the blazing late-August sunshine. It glinted off the lake to one side, while hills dominated the landscape on the other sides. He heard laughter from the lake and saw a kayak nose into the bay. A horse whinnied from the stable area.

Then silence.

God? What do I do now?

He'd felt like God led him to buy the Fosters' house. He wasn't about to clear their debt and let them continue the same bad habits with no consequences. The liens against their home had been paid, though, leaving them with a small amount of cash. Had he expected Cadence to be grateful? To understand immediately why he'd done it?

Out of love.

He was terrible at expressing emotion. Grandfather had challenged him on that, asking how what he felt for Cadence differed from other female friends. He certainly wouldn't have spent this much money bailing out anyone else, knowing he'd never see a penny of it again.

Thanks to being a Sullivan — through no effort of his own — he could drop the cash in one go and not hurt.

Graham sank into a wooden Adirondack chair in the

shade. He'd also done nothing to earn God's favor or all the benefits that came from being a child of God.

God loved him incredibly more than he could ever love Cadence or anyone else. A massive wave of gratitude rolled over him and brought tears prickling to his eyes. He'd never felt all the privilege in his life quite so fully as in that moment.

God had blessed him far more than he could imagine in his earthly family and, far more, in his heavenly family.

WHAT HAD JUST HAPPENED?

Cadence stared at the door Graham had exited. He'd offered to buy her parents' house and give it to her.

Was he some kind of crazy?

There was no other reason he'd do something that extravagant.

Unless he loved her. Like, really truly adored her with all the single-minded focus with which a man could love a woman. And that couldn't be true. Could it?

He didn't talk or act like a man in love, but he definitely kissed like it.

Her lips tingled at the memory of the single kiss they'd shared. She'd started it, sure, but he'd gotten into the spirit of it in less than a split second. She wanted more, but everything was so complicated.

Mom's gambling. Dad's coverup. Paul's pursuit.

Graham offered a way out that had never occurred to her, probably because she couldn't simply cough up a cool mil or two any old day of the week without breaking a sweat. Did it even set Graham back in a way he'd notice? Would he have to make payments, or was the purchase a blip on his radar?

How could she accept his offer?

How could she not?

Right. She'd told her parents she'd pay them back for the wedding costs. If she sold the house Graham gifted her, she could do that and still... no. That wasn't what Graham was doing this for. It wouldn't take that kind of cash to pay off their debts. Twenty or thirty grand and she'd be clear.

Besides, if she sold the house, her parents would have to move out, and then what? Did she care if they saved face? They'd keep guilting her until she at least bought them a less pretentious house in a cheaper part of the city.

She'd never be free of the weight. Family wasn't supposed to be a burden, especially not one's parents. Weren't they supposed to take care of their kids, not the other way around? At least, until old age came along, but Daniel and Amelia Foster were in their mid fifties. It should have been many years yet before Cadence felt compelled to shoulder their care.

Now she had another option, and it was already in motion. If she did nothing, Graham would buy her parents' house — maybe he already had — and give her the deed, and she could let them keep living there. Should they pay her rent? What if Mom kept gambling?

This was too hard. She detested all her options. She'd called Graham here to accept his awkward marriage proposal, but he hadn't let her get that far before implying she could bypass marriage and still get the benefits from him.

The financial benefits. Not the personal ones.

Because he regretted his previous offer and had found a way out of it that still salved his conscience. That's all it was. He probably kissed dozens of women the way he'd kissed her.

At least, if they initiated it.

No, that wasn't right. She'd have heard rumors if he'd been dating, and he wasn't the kind of guy to kiss without some kind of real interest.

Graham cared about her. Obviously, or he wouldn't be buying her parents' house to give her — and them — a fresh start.

But caring for someone wasn't enough. It wasn't the same thing as love for a lifetime. People cared for friends. Cared for pets.

He'd rejected her. He'd bought her off. So now she was free to go wherever she wanted and find a new job, a new home, a new purpose. One that didn't include being Paul's wife or working for Bradley Consortium. One that didn't include Sweet River Ranch, either.

Tears flooded her eyes. She didn't want to leave this place. Paisley was a truer friend to her in two short months than any of her Chicago friends, even her chosen maid of honor. She'd hung out more with Kaci and Heather and Emma and the other resort staff than with her previous friends.

Cadence could start over somewhere else, but she didn't want to. Not really. Walter Sullivan was a fair boss who ran a tight ship. There was a camaraderie here between the staff. The living conditions were solid if not phenomenal.

But could she stay and see Graham every day if he never returned her love the way she dreamed of?

She gripped the back of the chair, grounding herself back into the resort's conference room.

Exactly how did she dream of Graham loving her?

More kisses. More slow, intimate smiles. More... everything.

Her cheeks warmed at the pictures forming in her mind. He seemed so sure she wouldn't want him that he'd given her an out with no strings attached. But... what would prove to him that she wanted him with or without strings?

It wasn't because of his bank account or the fact that he could buy a mansion without blinking. It wasn't because he was a Sullivan. It was because beneath his awkwardness was a heart of gold, a heart that seemed to beat for her, though he seemed unable to believe it could be reciprocated.

Okay, fine. She had a mission. How to convince him they could build a love and a bond for a lifetime?

CHAPTER TWENTY

The atmosphere in the dining room fairly shimmered with something Graham couldn't define. Aunt Nadine beamed the biggest smile he'd ever seen on her face. A quick glance around the space revealed a glowering Weston. Nothing new to see there. Jude wasn't present.

Hmm. Graham picked his choices from the sandwich and salad bar. Nadine made the best sourdough rolls he'd ever tasted. He'd sure miss those if — when — he returned to Chicago.

He hadn't heard anything further from Cadence in the couple of days since they'd talked. Since he'd blown it yet again, because he seemed incapable of anything else. Now she came into the dining room flanked by Paisley and Kaci.

Graham's gut clenched at the smile on her face. Nice someone was happy, because he definitely was not.

He heaped smoked roast beef onto his bun then added pasta salad as well as sliced tomatoes and cucumbers to his plate. Good thing he was working out, even though it was only jogging on the ranch lanes in the early mornings. So far, no one but a few guests had caught him, and they weren't telling.

"Over here, Graham!" Bryce called.

Graham set his plate down across from his cousin and glanced around. "Any idea what's going on?"

Bryce's eyebrows ratcheted up. "Going on? Besides that this is the last full weekend of summer coming up?"

"Technically, summer doesn't end until September twenty-sec—"

"For all practical purposes, it ends Labor Day," Bryce cut in. "What do you mean by going on? Because Grandfather looks like the cat who swallowed a canary and then got a bellyache from it."

Graham swiveled around. "He's in the dining room? He never eats in here."

"Almost never," Bryce corrected. "Nadine usually has one of the girls run a tray to the office or to his suite, but if he's going to show, it's at lunch."

The old man sat with his back to the expansive windows overlooking the lake and watched the main lodge doors between every bite. And Bryce's description wasn't far off.

Graham's gaze narrowed. "I wonder…"

"Hmm?" Bryce took a giant bite of his sandwich as Maxwell set his tray down between them.

Nadine glanced at her phone, tucked it in her pocket, then said something to the kitchen helpers. She came out from behind the counter and crossed the space to Grandfather.

He looked up at her, and she patted him on the shoulder before they both focused on the lodge doors.

Graham followed their gaze as the doors opened and Jude entered holding the arm of a little old lady.

Eleanor.

Who else could she be?

She was tall and thin, wearing a navy and white tunic over navy slacks and sensible shoes. Her white hair was short and styled, and chunky navy earrings dangled from her ears. She stopped. Stared.

Grandfather rose to his feet and brushed his hand through his full head of hair as though expecting to find a bowler to doff. His gaze riveted to hers, and he stood glued to the spot, just as she did. They stared, no doubt sizing each other up.

Graham was vaguely aware that the buzz of the dining hall droned on unabated, even as he set his own sandwich down to watch the drama unfold.

"Who's that?" Maxwell asked, frowning.

"Eleanor. It can't be anyone else."

"Takes a lot of courage for her to come into the Sullivan den," Bryce observed.

"I think Nadine talked her into it. And maybe she feels safer here in a semi-public place where she can easily escape if she's uncomfortable."

"Escape?"

"Look at Jude. He's ready to scoop her up and make a run for it if Grandfather makes a wrong move."

Bryce laughed. "I can totally see that." He parked his own sandwich and crossed his arms. "Think we'll get an intro?"

"Probably? If the first few minutes go well, anyway." And it didn't escape Graham's notice that Dad and Uncle James weren't present for this momentous occasion. No doubt they'd present a layer Eleanor wasn't quite ready for. Would she want to meet Grandfather's other grandsons if not her half-brothers?

Maxwell's elbow jabbed Graham's ribs. "Weston doesn't look too happy."

Bryce rolled his eyes. "Dude hasn't smiled in his entire life."

Nadine took Grandfather by the arm and walked beside him to Jude and the woman. From this angle, Graham couldn't see Grandfather's face, but he could see Eleanor's as her eyes searched his. It took a moment for any sort of smile to cross her face, and then only as the old man bowed over the hand he'd taken in his.

Graham dared take a breath as Grandfather straightened, still holding her hand.

"Do we want them to revive their relationship?" Maxwell asked quietly. "What if he falls in love with her all over again?"

Graham's brain hadn't stretched quite that far. Was there any reason an eighty-year-old couldn't remarry? None he could think of. Not that he wanted to let his mind linger there for even a fraction of a second. Grandmother had passed away a decade ago, and Grandfather had made no effort to find his long-lost flame since then. He'd never dated that Graham had heard of, just poured himself into the company.

"Cool by me." Bryce shrugged. "Maybe he'd be less of a taskmaster if he had something else to distract him."

"He's mellowed out a lot since we came to Montana," Max countered.

Which was also true, but they had Tate to thank for that. It was Tate who'd shortened their office hours, eliminated evening crew meetings, and put Grandfather on a tether. Still, the old man had gone along with it all.

Grandfather turned slightly and surveyed the dining room. When his gaze landed on his grandsons, he beckoned.

"Showtime, boys," Bryce said. "Let's go meet her."

"Maybe we can scare her off," Max muttered. "I'm not sure this is a good idea."

Graham rose along with his cousins, and the trio wended between the tables to where the foursome stood near the entrance. Weston came from over by the windows, as Tate, Stephanie, and Jamie entered the lodge doors in time to converge with the rest.

"I'd like you to meet my family, Eleanor. Boys, this is Nadine's mother, Eleanor." Grandfather's Adam's apple bobbed when he swallowed. "The woman I wronged so many years ago."

Eleanor patted his arm. "We were both in the wrong. Now, tell me who's who, and all about this adorable toddler."

Graham waited his turn for the introduction, aware of Weston's taciturn presence at his back. Was the cowboy afraid the Sullivan guys would encroach on his grandmother? Or might he agree with Maxwell, that nothing good could come of this reunion?

"THAT GUY IS SUCH A WET BLANKET."

Cadence got the impression that Paisley had barely been able to hold back her opinion in the dining room, but kudos to her — she'd managed. Also, she didn't need to ask whom her roommate referred to. Or what the situation had been.

How to respond, then? "Maybe Weston felt that was a lot to throw at them without warning."

"Oh, I'm sure he knew. His mom was beaming all morning, Jude was missing, and Mr. Grouchy Face was scowling worse than usual. Which is saying something. So, yeah, he had to know what was coming down the pipeline."

"I think it's sweet that Mr. Sullivan and his long-lost love have reunited."

"They had an affair."

"I know. But still, a lot of years have gone by. They've both been married and widowed. So, I'm going to stick to sweet."

"Weston doesn't agree with you."

Cadence stopped so suddenly that Paisley ran into her. "Why do you care?"

"I *don't* care. The guy's a jerk."

"You've spent the entire summer trying to make him smile."

"And have not succeeded. Did I tell you I've accepted a job teaching skiing lessons in Vail this winter?"

Cadence blinked at the sudden change of topic. "Um, no. You did not. I thought you were planning to stay here all winter."

"I considered it." Paisley stepped around her and continued up the ranch lane.

Cadence fell into step beside her. Enlightenment began seeping in. "You thought you'd stay if you could get Weston to respond."

"Nah."

"You rejected that a little too quickly."

"I'm not letting that sour so-and-so rule my life."

"I'm hearing a lot of protest."

Paisley sent her a hard glare. "Do you have any idea how hard it is to be upbeat all the time?"

"I can't say that I do. I'm not as anti-social as what's-his-name, but I also don't try to be Lady Sunbeam. I am who I am."

"Which is closer to grumpy than happy, at least lately."

Cadence sighed. "You're probably right. You know the saying about jumping out of the frying pan into the fire? I feel more like I'm jumping from one frying pan to another to keep out of the fire. But my feet are still getting scorched."

"Let's talk about that."

"Any topic besides Weston, huh?" Cadence hid her grin.

Paisley rolled her eyes. "For *sure*. Listen. I think you should get Graham to notice you. I know he likes you, but he doesn't quite know what to do about it. He's a little obtuse at times."

Her roommate had no idea what Graham had already done — Mom had freaked out that an anonymous someone had bought their house out of receivership with permission to stay living in it with minimal rent. He hadn't mentioned the rent part to Cadence, but it made sense. Mom had enough to pay off her debt and the wedding with not much left over, but that was more than they deserved.

Paul had sent her a nasty message saying never mind, she could consider his offer of marriage irrevocably off the table and not to come begging to him anymore.

As if she ever had. Cadence had sighed with relief. She was free. Sort of. She still owed Graham, but he wasn't going to accept anything from her.

"So, Graham."

Cadence glowered at her roommate as they walked toward staff housing. "Hmm? I'm not sure I trust your help. Or if I even want it."

"Of course, you trust me." Paisley rubbed her hands together. "You need a new social media hashtag or two. True love at SRR, maybe. Or start sticking hearts in the corners of your images. Or..."

"You're crazy."

Paisley shrugged. "But it might work. You know he follows the resort on all the sites. You can send him a message no one else will pick up. Except me and anyone else in the know."

"I'm not going to send him secret messages on social media. That's... lame."

"Got a better idea?"

Talking to him in the conference room hadn't worked. He was too focused on his own agenda, on his solid belief that she wasn't truly interested in him but only desperate for relief from her overwhelming problems. He'd provided a way out that didn't involve hearts.

But her heart was already involved. If she were honest, it had been since that night he'd arrived on her doorstep dripping with pool water.

Maybe Paisley was on to something. She needed to send Graham a message that he couldn't interrupt. Where he couldn't second-guess their interactions. Where time and perseverance would reveal her heart to him.

And not with a heart in the corner of every social media image, either. How tacky would that be?

She glanced at Paisley, walking along beside her. "Okay, so let's talk about social media. But I definitely need better ideas than you've come up with so far."

"Ooh! Let's make an idea board and do some brainstorming. This sounds fun."

Fun wasn't the word Cadence would have come up with, but she'd go along with it for now. Paisley had an overactive imagination, and maybe this would put it to good use. At least, Cadence could glean from her ideas and reject the ones that were way over the top. It wasn't like she had to fulfill Paisley's agenda.

Maybe she should make her own scheme to keep Paisley at Sweet River over the winter. Because if all went well, Cadence wasn't going anywhere herself. Of course, if it went poorly, maybe she'd need a job in Vail, too. Maybe Paisley would let her tag along.

Paisley tapped her jaw thoughtfully as they strolled along the road.

Cadence sent a prayer heavenward. Was it okay to pursue Graham blatantly? She'd been studying biblical love the past week or two. She'd come to the conclusion that Paul's attitude toward her had never resembled God's love in any way at all.

But someone who was willing to buy a house for her

that neither of them would likely ever live in… that was an act of love.

Even if Graham wasn't ready to acknowledge it yet.

CHAPTER TWENTY-ONE

G raham hated how fervently he stalked the Sweet River Ranch social media accounts. Cadence hadn't uploaded a lot of selfies since the early days, but it was still a chance to see the ranch resort through her eyes. To imagine what the rest of the growing number of followers saw.

It only took a couple of minutes a few times a day. She took her job seriously, so there was usually something new to see.

Had she had a chat with Grandfather? Because the tone of her posts had changed slightly with more behind-the-scenes stuff. There was Grandfather leaning back in his office chair, hands linked behind his head. He wasn't exactly smiling, but he seemed more approachable than he often did. The list of hashtags seemed to go on and on. Graham's vision blurred — pretty sure it wasn't that he wore smudged glasses — with the list that included #SweetRiverRanch #owner #come2Montana and at least a dozen more.

Later that afternoon, an image popped up of Jude fixing a tap with a look of focus on his face. Some of the same hashtags had been listed, but there were others. #renovation #restoration

Graham rolled his eyes. If Cadence was trying to get people to #come2Montana, she needed to find staff who smiled and looked welcoming. Which counted him out. He'd forgotten how to smile lately, if he'd ever known how.

Had he misunderstood her? Because he hadn't quite figured out the reason she'd called him to the conference room two days ago. He'd jumped to conclusions — that quick brain of his could be a liability — and she'd shut him down in three seconds flat.

She hadn't even seemed relieved about the house. About her freedom to make her own choices.

He wanted her to choose him. Not because he'd erased the threats over her, but because she loved him.

Graham had created a grand gesture to show his love, and it had backfired. Or maybe fizzled. What could he have done differently? Just grabbed her in his arms and kissed her?

He froze, still staring at Jude's face on the phone in his hand. Maybe that's exactly what he should have done. It would have prevented him from saying more things to be misconstrued. It would have prevented her from talking, too. He liked the sound of her voice — he did — but he liked the sensation of her lips against his even better.

His eyes shuttered as he relived the amazing kiss from weeks ago now. Why couldn't they do that again and again? Why did his awkwardness have to mess everything up?

"Sleeping on the job?"

Graham's eyes sprang open, and he shoved his glasses up his nose to see his grandfather better. "No, sorry. Thinking."

The old man's gaze narrowed at him. "Deep thoughts, by the looks of it."

"Have you ever been misunderstood because you didn't know how to make your thoughts clear?" As the words came out of Graham's mouth, he winced. Of course not. Grandfather was smooth, a born leader, good in front of people with never a hint of awkwardness.

Grandfather lowered himself into his desk chair and swiveled it to face Graham. "All the time."

"Really?"

He chuckled. "Yes, of course. I spent so many years focusing on Sullivan Enterprises that I honed my business acumen to the detriment of my personal skills. I have many regrets. Most of them have to do with your grandmother."

Did Graham even want to know? But it seemed important to.

"I loved her. I did. But I rarely showed her that truth in a way she could find comfort in. I wanted to provide a life of ease, and I succeeded. I wanted her to have the best of everything. The house, the travel, the social niceties. I would have given her the moon on a platter if it had been at all possible."

Graham nodded. He felt the same stirrings to offer everything to Cadence that Grandfather described. He'd already done what he could — maybe more than he ought — to free her to make her own choices.

"What she wanted was me." Grandfather looked down

at his hands clenched in his lap. "I didn't think I was that great. I was sure I knew better, that she'd appreciate a whirlwind trip to Greece more than a quiet week with me. She'd see me for who I was. A man focused on business and unable to access his emotions."

"I'm not sure I want to hear more."

Grandfather leaned forward on his elbows, his gaze skewering Graham's. "And for that reason, I think you need to, boy. Because I see a lot of me in you."

"Not so, sir." Graham shook his head. "Tate, maybe, or even Bryce. They have an easy way about them, a confidence like yours. I... I don't have that. I understand numbers, but people? Not at all."

"Confidence can be faked."

Maybe, but Graham wasn't persuaded any of the Sullivan men were doing so. Even Dad and Uncle James exuded innate composure. Could they all be pretenders, but everyone else faked better than he did? It wasn't possible.

"I see you don't believe me. But the real point is how you love. I let your grandmother down, boy. I figured it out, at least somewhat, in the last few years before her passing. After that, to fill my emptiness, I did the only thing I knew how, and that was pour myself back into the business and take you boys with me."

Graham had seen the evidence, so he cautiously nodded.

"I've pushed everyone as hard as I've pushed myself. My sons. All you boys. I'm sorry."

Graham blinked and refocused on the old man. "Sorry? For what?"

"For making any of you think that money was more important than relationships. That hotels mattered so much. You know that story Jesus told about how hard it is for the rich to enter the kingdom of God? It's true. I've seen it in so many associates in my circles. We feel we are self-made. That we don't need anyone, that God is a myth or, if He isn't, we don't need Him, anyway. We treat ourselves like gods."

Huh. Graham needed to think on that.

"But what is most telling is how we treat those we love. 1 John 4 tells us, 'Beloved, let us love one another, for love is from God, and whoever loves has been born of God and knows God.' It goes on to explain what that love looks like: 'In this the love of God was made manifest among us, that God sent his only Son into the world, so that we might live through him.' And what was Jesus like?"

It seemed the old man awaited a reply.

"You mean besides dying for us."

Grandfather nodded.

"Well, He spent time with people. Healing them, teaching them about His kingdom, simply... being with them."

"Right. He wasn't hung up on estate planning or on the size of His nonexistent house. His vacations took Him to mountaintops to pray for maybe a few hours before the crowds found Him again. I doubt His clothing looked any better than the next guy's."

Graham envisioned a first-century Jewish man just going around loving people.

"Beloved," Grandfather quoted softly. "If God so loved us, we also ought to love one another."

If a guy was talking about grand gestures to show love, hadn't Jesus acted out the greatest one of all? He'd given His very life so that others could live. Others like Graham halfway around the globe in the twenty-first century.

How could he possibly love Cadence a fraction as much?

And what good was a grand gesture without the love?

CADENCE POINTED her camera at the head wrangler. "Say cheese!"

Weston glowered at her. "I don't smile."

"Would it kill you to try?"

"It might. What are you doing, anyway? Who cares about me? I'm only a cog in a random wheel around here."

"Everyone is important. Besides, you're one of the boss's grandsons. People want to see your face." She stared him down. "Your smiling face."

"He'd have been as happy if he'd never heard of us. I don't know why my mother insisted on finding him."

Cadence let the camera hang from its strap around her neck. "Mr. Sullivan seems more contented lately than when I first came."

Weston snorted. "As if it's not enough to mess with Mom, Jude, and me, now he's after my grandmother. She doesn't deserve to be sucked into his vortex."

Which direction was he going with that statement? That Ms. Eleanor wasn't good enough for Mr. Sullivan? By his tone, she suspected the opposite. That his grandmother was better off without his grandfather.

Curiosity won out. "Are they going to keep seeing each other?"

"They'd better not."

"Why? They obviously once shared some—"

"He took advantage of her. She was his lowly secretary."

The elegant older woman didn't look like she'd ever been a lowly anything. "If she can forgive him, shouldn't we all do the same?" Not that Cadence had any personal investment in the matter.

"Someone needs to keep a cool head about them. My brother is all for a reunion. He's nuts."

"What do all your cousins think?"

Weston glowered at her. "The mighty Sullivans?"

"Your *cousins* Tate, Bryce, Maxwell, and Graham." She kept her voice level.

He shrugged. "Who knows? Who cares? They don't approve of me or Jude. They'd definitely be happier without us in the picture."

"Tate met the love of his life out here in Montana. He'd never have come if it wasn't for your mom finding her father."

"Whatever."

There was more to Weston's hurt than his newfound extended family, but Cadence was in no position to probe deeper. She'd probably overstepped already, one of her best talents.

She held up her camera. "I need a few shots for social media."

Weston grunted. "Do whatever you have to do for a paycheck, I guess."

Did the man need to be so surly and keep everyone at

arm's length? And why had Paisley made it her personal mission to get him to relax and smile? It was a fool's agenda, and Paisley was no fool.

Never mind. "I do need my paycheck, as do you and everyone else. So, if you wouldn't mind…" She clicked the shutter. "I'd love some shots of you by the corral fence or up on Ranger."

"I'm not riding this morning."

"I know!" Cadence snapped her fingers. "How about if you stand talking to him?" She'd never seen the cowboy pleasanter than when he crooned to one of the horses.

"Fine, if it gets you off my back."

"Definitely. I'll only take up another ten or fifteen minutes of your time."

"Good, because I've got things to do before this afternoon's trail ride. Actual physical work."

Sounded like he was sniping at the Sullivan cousins for having office jobs. But Bryce worked as the groundskeeper. It wasn't like the guy never worked up a sweat or got dirt on him.

Weston exited the stable a few minutes later leading Ranger, then leaned on the corral fence beside the gelding. He even managed a neutral face, which was saying something.

She took some with her camera then, on a whim, some with her phone. "Thanks."

He narrowed his gaze. "You're finally done here?"

"Yes, sir."

"There's only one sir around here, and it's not me."

Cadence laughed. "Gotcha. But yes. Thanks for your

time. Is there room on today's trail ride? I haven't been out for a while."

"Sure. Whatever. I'll need to stick some beginner on Mirage, but Enchantment is too much of a handful for most of the greenhorns."

"Oooh, high praise! I love riding Enchantment. I'll be back at two, then."

"Suit yourself." He turned away.

Cadence shook her head as she watched him lead Ranger away, their heads close together. She snapped one more pic for good measure, then rolled through her captures.

Hmm. For all his surliness, he'd done all right in this photo shoot. His most negative expression had been pensiveness. She could work with that.

In fact…

Her thumbs flew across her phone as she texted Paisley.

> Hey, look who's not super grumpy today!

And then she sent two of the best photos and waited. It didn't take long for Paisley to respond.

> Yay for not grumpy. I wouldn't have believed it if you hadn't sent pix so I could see it with my own eyes. Couldn't get him to actually smile, huh?

Cadence chuckled.

> Nope. Not today. I'll leave that to you.

She held her breath, but Paisley didn't respond. Had she expected her to?

Cadence uploaded one to social media and tagged it with #ruggedcowboy #cowboycountry and #come4atrailride along with the usuals.

And now she was ready for Graham. Her heart pounded. How was she going to get him in his natural habitat and looking happier than Weston had? Because there was a distinct resemblance between the two cousins' resting expressions these days.

Sadness, tinged with despair.

Why couldn't Graham see who was right in front of him, looking for the love of a lifetime?

And maybe… ditto for Weston, but who was she to figure that out? She was having enough trouble with her own love life to try to interfere in other peoples'.

Much.

CHAPTER TWENTY-TWO

Graham pulled up the year-to-date spreadsheets for all of the Sullivan Enterprises hotels. Grandfather would be asking for the numbers through the end of August by sometime tomorrow, and Graham's job was to make sure everything was collated.

"Heading to the dining room?" Tate stretched at his desk.

"In a few." Graham stared at his screen, though his eyes blurred. His contacts had been bugging him lately, but things weren't much clearer with his glasses. Maybe he should see his optometrist next time he was in Chicago. Whenever that would be.

"See you there." Tate exited the space, leaving Graham in peace.

Cadence hadn't been at her desk lately when he was present, and there was no evidence she'd cruised through in the off hours. He glanced at her darkened corner, wishing against wish that he knew what to do, that they could get past this awkward spot.

The door cracked open, and she breezed in, carrying her camera. "Ah, Tate said I'd find you here."

Graham blinked. Tate told her? That was a laugh. Where else did she think he'd be during office hours?

"Can I get a couple of shots for social media? I'm doing a series of behind-the-scenes posts so our followers can see there's more than the glitz."

Glitz? People thought a ranch was glamorous? He leaned back in his chair and studied her face. There was nothing to see. No passion. Nothing personal at all. His heart plummeted in his chest. Had he read too much into everything? Maybe he'd misunderstood all along, and she'd only been messing with him.

"Uh, I guess so. What do you want me to be doing?" Kissing her wasn't out of the question, though a photo of that might be awkward on social media. Whatever. Bring it.

"Just focus on your screen. I promise I won't capture anything on it that should be kept private."

Good thing the spreadsheets were up, not the Sweet River Ranch social pages, or she'd know he'd been stalking her.

He forced a smile. "You mean, focus on work like I always do."

"Exactly." She raised her camera.

Fine. They could get this out of the way, and then they'd talk. Or kiss. Or both. In either order.

He managed an impassive stare at the monitor while she clicked away.

"Now look at me as though you just noticed me."

Graham turned slightly, and his eyes drank in the sight

of her as she raised her camera again. "You're beautiful," he blurted out.

"Thanks." But her voice was muffled. "There, that will do for now. Thank you."

He surged to his feet. "Cadence."

She paused by the door, her back to him. "What?"

Here went nothing. "I lo—"

The door swung open and crashed into her, breaking what might have been a moment… but probably wouldn't have been.

Grandfather stopped in midstride, his shrewd gaze swinging from one of them to the other. "Am I interrupting something?"

"No!" Cadence darted out the door and disappeared down the corridor.

Graham sank back into his chair. "Probably not."

"Explain."

"She came to take photos of me for her social media project. But she seemed in a hurry to get her job done and get out of here."

The old man sighed. "Pardon my bad timing, and go after her."

There'd been no spark. Those few minutes had been like he'd been in Paisley's presence. Or his mother's. Well, *he'd* had spark, obviously, but Cadence hadn't let a glimmer of it out, which meant it probably didn't exist.

She'd been taking him for a ride all this time?

But she'd kissed him.

"Boy? You're overthinking this."

Probably true. He met his grandfather's gaze. "I'm so bad at this."

His grandsire thumbed toward the door. "Practice makes perfect."

Or gave him one more opportunity to make a fool of himself. Wasn't it time he risked everything, though? Because he couldn't get her out of his mind, and it was making him heartsick, consuming every thought, every minute. Even his prayers these days seemed to focus on Cadence unless he forced them elsewhere.

He tried. He did. And he needed to get to the bottom of whatever this thing between them was. But… now?

Grandfather stood beside the open door, his eyebrows raised. "Well?"

"Pray for me." Graham stood on shaky legs and headed for the door.

Did he think the old man would laugh at that? Because he didn't. Instead, he grasped Graham's shoulder. "Father God, I commit Graham to You right now. I pray that You will fill him with the peace only You can give, the love only You can give, and the joy only You can give. May Your will be done, in Jesus' name, amen." He patted Graham's back. "Go on."

Graham stepped into the corridor and turned toward the common areas. The chatter of voices and the clatter of utensils and plates reminded him it was lunch time, as though the fragrant aroma of beef stew wouldn't have been enough to alert him on its own.

He faltered at the edge of the dining room, taking in the line snaking past the counter. Cadence then Paisley turned with loaded trays toward the staff table they often frequented at the far side of the space. Dozens of diners surrounded the round tables in between them. Tate, Stephanie, and Jamie sat at one with Jude and Bryce.

Would there be room at Cadence's table? He could sit with his cousins if not. No, it was time — past time — for him to get over his discomfiture and make absolutely certain Cadence knew how he felt. Was the middle of the bustling dining room a good idea, though? At least, she couldn't run without making a scene. If there would be a scene, it would be because they were kissing.

Graham swallowed hard as he inched forward in line, a family from Kansas chatting in front of him about this afternoon's trail ride. How could anyone be this excited about sitting on top of that much restless power? Would those kids be safe? What if...?

No. Graham was done with fear. Completely done. Maybe he should see if there was room on the trail ride. That was one excuse Grandfather would embrace for why Graham was late with the numbers. Not that he would be. There wasn't that much left to double check.

He scanned the room for Weston but saw no sign of him. Fine. He'd stop by the stable after lunch and find out then.

Kaci, Heather, and Maxwell took the last three seats at Cadence's table.

Didn't that just figure? Either way, he needed to eat.

"There's Cadence," the girl in front of him said in whispered awe.

"The social media manager?" her mom asked. "The one who posted about the trail ride?"

Graham's ears perked.

"Yeah, that's her! The hashtags were about 'trail ride at

two' and 'join me,' so I hope she's going. Maybe we'll make it into one of her posts! Wouldn't that be cool? I could show all my friends. They'll be so jealous."

The mother smiled. "It will be fun whether she goes or not. I can't believe summer is almost over and you two are back to school Tuesday."

The girl grimaced. "Don't remind me."

If he'd had any doubt about that trail ride, he was definitely going now, unless there wasn't a spare horse. Strangely, he hoped that wasn't the case.

Also, how had he missed one of Cadence's social media posts?

"He's here," Paisley hissed in her ear.

"Shh." Cadence glanced around the table as Heather dropped her tray beside her. "I saw him."

"Hey, everyone!" Kaci claimed the spot beside Heather, while Maxwell was already chatting with the two guys from the landscaping crew who'd been here first.

"Hi!" Cadence forced a smile and tried not to notice Graham across the space where he shifted from one foot to the other and back again in the lineup behind a family she'd seen around for the past few days.

"There are only a couple of more groups to check out of the cottages on Firefly Lane, then we're closing access for the season, so we can finalize the renovations." Heather nodded in satisfaction.

"Give me a heads up to get all the linens out of there," Kaci said. "Oh, and the kitchen stuff."

"We'll get a crew to haul all that to the storage areas," Heather promised. "It's nice not having people around. I mean, I get that's the purpose, and they pay our bills, but man it will be nice to roll without tourists in the way."

Cadence only had one more week of the term she'd promised Walter Sullivan. She needed to make an appointment to talk to him about more — or not — but she kept hoping something might spark yet with her and Graham, and that would make things clearer.

Of course, she'd been a chicken when she took photos a bit ago, and whatever Graham had been about to say had been completely disrupted by the boss's entrance. Never mind. She'd get her next post up and maybe he'd see... at least if he was actually following the page as closely as it seemed.

Meanwhile, she'd focus on getting more shots during the trail ride.

Graham's gaze latched onto hers across the dining room, and she forced her attention past him to the great room beyond.

He turned toward the table where his cousins sat, carrying his tray.

There was still one spot there, right next to his. She could grab her things and walk over. She could make a move.

But hadn't she made enough of them already? When did it become time for him to do the pursuing?

Her conscience niggled. Was that what he'd done by buying her parents' house? The magnanimity of that totally overwhelmed her, rendering her speechless. But he hadn't said he'd done it because he loved her. He'd made sure she knew he'd done it to free up her choices.

Was one of those possible choices Graham? Was that what he'd been hinting at?

Well, she'd post his photos online, throw in a few hashtags, and sit back and wait. If he didn't make a move in the next day or two, what would she do? It wasn't like she didn't know where he lived, though knocking on a single guy's door in the late evening when his lights finally appeared didn't seem like the wisest choice.

She bit back a snort. Like Graham would take advantage of her. She'd always had to be on guard with handsy Paul, but not with Graham.

Cadence turned to Paisley. "Riding this afternoon?"

"Nope, definitely not." Paisley wrinkled her nose. "We've got enough kids around this week for a scavenger hunt. You'll want some photos of that."

"Can you take a few and text them to me if I don't get back in time? I'm trail riding."

"Traitor," Paisley muttered.

Cadence elbowed her lightly. "Speak up. I can't hear you."

Paisley couldn't hold a frown for long. "Have a good time, okay? Seriously? But also seriously—" she lowered her voice "—give that cowboy a kick in the rear for me if you get a chance."

"Totally an example of opposites attract."

"In your dreams."

"Maybe in yours?" What Paisley saw in Weston, Cadence couldn't imagine. Probably nothing more than the ultimate challenge. Gleeful extroverts like Paisley took grumpy introverts like Weston as a personal affront.

Or maybe it was more.

Like Cadence was a master of romantic interaction. Look at her and Graham dancing around each other, each apparently as unsure as the other one.

For better or for worse, this was going to end.

She glanced over as he left his table, scraping much of his meal into the trash as he went by. She frowned. That was unusual. Guys, even geeky ones like Graham, rarely let anything get between them and food, and Nadine's recipes were on par with the best.

He exited the area through the main lodge doors, not down the corridor to the office.

Cadence frowned. Where was he going, if not back to work? That's all he ever did, make numbers troop in tidy columns. *The ants go marching two by two. Hurrah, hurrah.* She pushed the lyrics from the children's song out of her mind.

Okay, fine. She had barely enough time to finish her own lunch, upload the photos of Graham, pray over the best hashtags, and get to the stable to saddle up by two o'clock.

She tuned back in to hear Maxwell, Heather, and Jordan debate the pros and cons of real stone countertops versus imitation in the rental units. Like that was something she cared about. Not.

Paisley and Kaci commiserated about a particularly difficult family whose kids had been wild monsters and whose parents had left the unit a shambles when they checked out yesterday.

Checked out. Cadence had already checked out in her mind. She stared down at the stew and the sourdough bun slathered with melting butter. She took a couple of bites, but it wasn't sitting well. Probably nerves.

Maybe that's what it had been for Graham, too. Was he as nervous as she was as the summer drew to a close? Did he care as much as she did about the future, or did he think his purpose in her life was over now that she was free to choose?

Hogwash.

If she were free to choose, she wanted to choose him. But... what if that wasn't what he wanted?

CHAPTER TWENTY-THREE

Y ou're here to *ride?*" Weston's eyebrows disappeared into the shadow of his cowboy hat. He made a show of peering past Graham. "I don't see anyone twisting your arm."

Graham braced himself and smiled, though it nearly killed him. "If you have a spare horse. It's a beautiful day, and I haven't taken much time to enjoy it lately."

"Sure. I believe that. You're only here because Cadence signed up."

"Oh, did she? I didn't know that when I decided." Which was entirely true.

"You're not fooling anyone. But, yeah, if you think you can handle Ranger, you can go."

"Uh... that's your horse."

"Good observation."

"Aren't you going?"

"Not today. Tyler is leading the group, and he's got his own mount."

Ranger was... restless. He was taller than most of the

others and moved with a barely contained energy. He was more horse than Graham was prepared to handle.

"You afraid of him?"

"Maybe a little?"

Weston rolled his eyes. "Dude, you're afraid of everything. Of the kayaks. Of the hills. Of little itty-bitty snakes." He leaned closer. "Of Cadence."

The snakes weren't itty-bitty. Graham might not have seen one in real life, but he'd seen photos, and that was enough. Someone had told him they weren't as likely to be spotted this time of year, though.

Okay, fine. He was afraid of a lot of things, but that was changing. Right? He would man up. In addition to jogging, he'd already lifted weights twice in the resort's gym, late in the evening when no one else was around. Light weights, but still, they were something.

"If you think I can handle Ranger, I'm in."

Was that respect glimmering in Weston's eyes? Possibly humor, but that couldn't be, because the cowboy had no funny bone.

"Go inside and talk to him for a bit. See what you think."

"Okay." Graham's knees quaked.

"He likes carrots."

Graham paused in the doorway of the stable to allow his eyes to adjust. He was early since he hadn't been certain there'd be a horse for him, so he had time to get to know Ranger.

Or time to chicken out.

He glanced over his shoulder, but Weston had disappeared. Graham pulled his phone out of his pocket and checked social media.

There he was, all focused on the computer screen with a little frown on his face. Was this truly the best shot Cadence had taken? Was this what he looked like to her, all serious and focused and... But that's who he was. He couldn't help it.

His eyes swept the hashtags. Most were familiar, but his heart hammered when he found the ones unique to this post. #thebrainsbehindSRR #geeksRgreat #swoon #isit-truelove

Wait. What?

Graham's feet all but welded to the stone floor of the stable's alleyway. Was Cadence saying what it sounded like she was saying? He scanned them again as all of time seemed to stand still, right down to the flecks of dust in the sunbeams stretching in front of him.

Hashtag is it true love? Was she declaring herself to him? Via social media?

He hadn't given her a chance to do it in person, but she hadn't tried. Even an hour ago, she'd been in his office. They'd been alone, at least until Grandfather barged in. Graham would like to think he'd have followed through with the declaration he'd begun. 'I love you' had been on the tip of his tongue. It had even half been spoken before Grandfather burst in.

Suddenly, Graham felt twelve feet tall, almost too colossal to ride teeny-tiny Ranger without his knees dragging on the trail. He could absolutely manage that puny horse. He could tackle a mountain lion and tear it apart with his bare hands like King David had purported to do in his youth.

If it turned out Cadence wasn't riding this afternoon, after all, that was fine. Graham would conquer his giants one at a time. First came the horse, then her. Now, where was the basket of carrots Weston kept on hand?

INSTEAD OF RIDING, Cadence should track Graham down. She'd stopped by the office, but Mr. Sullivan only said Graham had taken the afternoon off.

That was unusual. Unheard of, really.

Since she couldn't spot him anywhere around the lodge or the grounds, she'd go riding as she'd planned. That would give him time to find her post.

That was the feeling of unease in her gut. She shouldn't have put her heart out there for the whole world to see, or at least the thousands of followers they'd amassed over the summer. Some of whom were right here on the property.

But what choice had she had when he shut her down every time she came nearby? Though he'd started a sentence that sounded suspiciously like 'I love you' before the boss had entered the office and wrecked the moment. And then she'd run like the chicken she was.

Cadence rolled her eyes as she headed up Pegasus Lane to where Weston and Tyler were already pairing up riders and mounts. Today's adventurers had all ridden before. She knew, because she'd been taking their photos.

Movement at the stable doorway caught her attention,

and she focused in that direction only to see Graham leading Ranger out.

She blinked. Looked again. She wasn't imagining things. Graham was here of his own free will? But he wasn't an experienced or confident rider, and Ranger was a handful, even for Weston.

Weston ran his hands over Ranger's tack as he chatted with Graham, then he nodded and stepped back.

Graham swung up to the saddle more smoothly than she expected. And that's when he noticed her standing there and staring at him with her mouth agape.

She snapped it shut, offered a thumbs-up, and shot off a few photos, in case she needed proof later. Then she entered the stable and found Enchantment and his tack. In only a few minutes, she led her mount out to the corral, too.

Tyrel nodded at her. "All right if I lead the group, and you bring up the rear?"

"Weston's not going?"

"Not today."

"Um, okay." That might mean this opportunity with Graham could be lost, but she was on the clock, so work came first. He'd understand that. It always did with him, too. Still, it felt like the universe continued to conspire against them.

She mounted Enchantment and gathered her reins as the guests, including the family from Kansas, plodded out behind Tyrel. Graham hung back, glancing furtively in her direction.

Her heart pounded. Had he seen the post? That was all

she wanted to know at the moment. Then she'd have a clue how to proceed.

Only the two of them were left. Sitting stiffly in his saddle, Graham followed the group, letting her do her job at the rear.

"Have fun." Weston's sardonic voice came from beside the gate as he prepared to close it behind her.

Eyebrows raised, Cadence looked him in the eye. "I think I will, thank you."

He chuckled and gestured up the trail with his chin. "Go on."

Graham glanced over his shoulder when the trail widened and nudged Ranger to one side.

They could ride side-by-side as they had on their first excursion. The time they'd agreed they both were interested. Seemed like they hadn't been on the same page for more than a few seconds at a time since then.

She kneed Enchantment up beside Ranger, who shied a little.

"Easy, boy," Graham murmured, patting the gelding.

Miraculously, Ranger settled. Maybe Graham would make a cowboy yet.

Cadence looked at him, trying to read his expression, but it was impossible. They rode together for what seemed forever but was likely only a few seconds before she blurted out, "What were you going to say to me when your grandfather walked into the office?"

Graham didn't answer.

She glanced over, and his eyes were scrunched tight. Then he opened them and met her gaze squarely. "I was going to say, 'I love you,' but I suspected it might not be what you want to hear."

Her throat thickened. "Really?"

"And I still don't know for sure if it's what you want to hear." He held her gaze for a few seconds longer before he let out a breath with a long whoosh. "Can we talk about it? Because I don't want either of us to ride off today without both of us knowing exactly where we stand with each other. If that's nowhere, I need to know, beyond a shadow of a doubt."

"Have you checked our social media in the past hour?"

He looked into her eyes. Nodded. "I don't want to assume I know what you meant with those tags, though. I'm not up on hashtag-speak."

Cadence licked her lips and observed his gaze drop when he noticed. She hadn't done it on purpose, but his reaction gave her hope. Bravery. "Which one? Swoon? Is it true love? Because I hoped that's what you had meant to say."

"I meant it." He repositioned himself slightly in the saddle while Ranger shifted agitatedly. "I love you, Cadence. Again, I don't know if—"

"I love you, Graham. It *is*, in fact, what I want to hear. I want to hear it a hundred thousand more times."

Graham nudged his glasses up his nose, his gaze never leaving hers. "I'm not sure I can fit that in today, but I'm game to try. Although, it might take a lifetime."

"I'm up for that." She stared back, trying to infuse her expression with all the assurance and, yes, even love that she could muster.

But Ranger swerved to the side of the trail, his ears flat back and his teeth bared.

"Graham!"

Screams came from around the bend, and an unholy stench flooded the air.

Skunk!

Ranger reared back, whinnying. But that was all Cadence had time to notice before Enchantment followed suit. It took all her focus to calm her mount and bring him to a standstill.

And that's when she realized Graham was lying crumpled on the trail and Ranger's hoofbeats were already fading. More horses surged toward them, and she jumped Enchantment into the fray to block Graham's body from the thundering hooves.

Wide-eyed, the family from Kansas and the other riders clung to their horses with clenched hands as they tore past on either side. Hopefully, the horses would slow as they returned to the corral. There wasn't anything Cadence could do about them now. Not while Graham lay unmoving on the hard dirt, his glasses lying at the edge of the trail.

Cadence slid off Enchantment as Tyler skidded to a stop. He grabbed her reins along with his as they both crouched beside Graham. "Is he okay? What happened?"

"Ranger happened." Cadence touched Graham's carotid artery and felt his strong pulse. "Graham, can you hear me?"

He groaned and shifted slightly. "What hit me?"

Tyler leaned in. "The ground, buddy. Falling knocked the wind out of you."

"I can't believe… I fell off."

"Not your fault. Ranger's got a thing about skunks since he got sprayed in the face last year. We haven't seen one around here since spring, though."

Cadence picked up Graham's eyeglasses. Amazingly, they didn't seem damaged. "You okay, sweetie?"

If Tyler gave her a strange look at the endearment, she could ignore him.

"Help me… sit up."

"You don't think anything's broken?" Tyler asked. "Wiggle your fingers and toes. Make sure."

Graham's fingers fluttered against the dirt. "Just winded, I think."

"We should call 9-1-1," Tyler went on. "I don't think you should move."

"I'm okay." Graham lifted himself to one elbow then both. "Nothing broken. I'm tougher than I look."

Tyler's arms hovered behind Graham's back as both men rose to their feet. "Don't sue the ranch if you're hurt. Or me."

"I won't." Graham flexed his shoulders slightly and winced. "Ranger bolted."

"He did." Tyler looked down the trail. "I should make sure everyone else made it safely back. Find out if anyone got hit directly with that spray. Ugh. There's not enough tomato juice in Montana to remove that stench."

"Go ahead," Cadence urged. "I'll stick with Graham. It's not far back."

"If you're sure." Tyler fingered the two horses' reins. "I'll take Enchantment back and send the wagon up?"

"Good idea," she said at the same time as Graham said, "No."

Tyler looked between them, sprang on his horse's back, and cantered down the trail, Enchantment following.

Graham wobbled on his feet, and Cadence wrapped both arms around him to keep him upright. He didn't need to meet the ground a second time in minutes.

"Are you sure you're okay?" she whispered against his chest.

"I am now." His arms came around her, his hands splayed across her back. "Where were we when we were so rudely interrupted?"

Cadence managed a chuckle, but it was going to take a long time before her heart rate came back to normal. "I told you I loved you, and it was so astounding that you fell off your horse."

"That's not exactly how I remember it."

"Oh? How's that?"

Graham tipped her chin back and looked deeply into her eyes through his smudged lenses. "I was going to stop the horse and get off so I could do this." He brushed his lips across hers.

Cadence didn't care about exploring the nuances anymore. Not when she stood in the arms of her beloved, and they both had kissing on their minds.

"Kiss me, Graham," she whispered. "I love you."

"I love you more." And his mouth claimed hers.

CHAPTER TWENTY-FOUR

The stench of skunk hovered over the ranch like a foul fog. In the lodge, Nadine simmered a vat of lemons on the stove, swearing that citrus helped counteract the smell. It worked. Sort of. At least, within the dining area.

Thankfully, none of the tourists had been hit directly by the spray.

Graham wasn't sure it could have been worse if they had. His nostrils burned even as he and Cadence sat on the edge of the dock that evening, bare feet dangling in the water.

No alligators. No crocodiles. Rattlesnakes and bears didn't swim. Did they? Maybe he didn't want to know.

He was going to cling to the assumption his feet were safe, because for the first time in his life, he felt like his heart was safe. Didn't that make all of him invulnerable? He'd felt like king of the universe mounting Ranger earlier. He felt ten times taller now.

Cadence leaned against his shoulder as long shadows stretched across the lake.

Graham barely dared breath at the brush of her hair against his arm, her floral scent barely discernible amid the sulfurous skunk odor. His skin thrilled to her nearness, and he closed his eyes as he rested his cheek against the top of her head.

"I like your beard," she murmured.

"You do?"

Cadence ran her fingers through the scruff and met his gaze. "I do."

One day, they'd say those words to each other. It was too soon for lifelong declarations, but wasn't that where they were heading? The calm assurance of that coming moment settled in his heart.

He lifted her fingers to his lips and kissed them, one at a time, holding her gaze steady with his own. "I love you."

"Ninety-nine thousand, nine hundred, ninety-two to go."

Graham couldn't help grinning. "You're going to keep count? I love you. I love you. I love you."

"You're a numbers guy." She giggled. "I thought you'd appreciate the effort."

He leaned down and swept her lips with his. "No need to keep score. There are many, many more where those came from. Like the stars in the night sky."

Cadence's fingers cradled his jaw. "There are way more stars visible here than I ever dreamed of in Chicago."

"There's way more love in my heart here than I ever dreamed of in Chicago."

She caressed his lips. "Me, too. I had no idea what love was. Not really."

"Paul?" He could only say his cousin's name because Graham was the guy who'd got the girl. Paul's loss for not knowing what treasure he had in his grasp. Graham's forever gain.

"Hmm, yes? But also, God's love. I was too busy, too distracted to think about it much until everything blew up."

Graham turned slightly to look out across the water as the evening breeze whispered over his face. A few lights shone in the cottages along the shore. A family of ducks paddled by amid the bullrushes. Peace. "Me, too. This summer has challenged me on every level, to be honest."

"You're a city boy on a ranch miles from anywhere."

"I was. Am I still a fish out of water? I don't know who I am."

Cadence shifted against his shoulder and looked up at him. "Are you thinking of staying in Montana?"

"What would you think about that?"

"You, first."

He managed a chuckle. How did she always nudge him to make the first move? "My life in Chicago feels very far away. I haven't been back since... well, since I met you. I didn't feel at home that weekend, either, but how much of that was because I was so unsettled about the wedding?"

"You were worried about me even before Paul proved his idiocy?"

His fingers tightened against her waist. "I've been aware of you since college."

"Right. But enough to be troubled?"

"I knew Paul wasn't good enough for you." Graham sighed. "I'm glad he proved it. Not sure your parents believe it yet, though." Did he dare ask how things had played out since he'd bought their house in Cadence's name?

"I'm not sure, either. I think they might come around. At least, Mom admitted to me she was the one gambling. She wanted so much to give me a fabulous society wedding and she just…" Cadence's voice broke.

Graham tugged her close as she wept into his chest. "I'm sorry. So sorry."

She sniffled. "It's not your fault."

"I know." Some days it seemed everything was his fault, but not this.

"But you helped fix it."

"I tried."

"You did more than try. What you did blows my mind away. I don't know what to do with a house in Hinsdale."

He managed a smile — not that she was looking — as he rubbed her shoulder. "It might come in handy someday. Or you can just let your parents live there."

"Mom's going into rehab."

That caught Graham's attention. "Really?" It was more than he'd hoped. He'd kind of figured he was throwing dollar bills into the void, but he'd done it for Cadence, not her parents, so it didn't matter.

"Next week. Dad finally pushed her to face up to the gambling."

"I'm so happy for them. For you."

Cadence dabbed at her eyes. "I hope it makes the difference long term."

"If they turn things over to God, it will."

"God." She offered a light chuckle. "Who knew He was so into our everyday business?"

"Grandfather has tried to drill that into my head. My mom and dad... a bit less so, though they took me to church growing up. They're kind of distracted these days with all the trappings. Busy-ness with the company. Keeping up appearances."

"My parents, too. They had money — less than you grew up with, for sure, but more than most. But the almighty dollar danced in front of them and made them forget everything else in pursuit of it."

Graham sat with the thought for a moment. Wasn't that what Grandfather had talked about the other day? How hard it was for a rich man to enter the kingdom of God because they felt they were self-made and didn't need God?

When all the trappings were stripped away, though, all people were equal in their need of God. Whether they were rich or poor, Black or white, educated or not... wasn't that what the Apostle Paul had said in Galatians?

There is neither Jew nor Greek, there is neither slave nor free, there is no male and female, for you are all one in Christ Jesus.

Graham had been surrounded by his bubble of privilege his entire life, while he had cousins who didn't know to whom they belonged. Somehow Eleanor had instilled her faith in God in Nadine, and Nadine had shared it with her sons. Was Weston a believer? Was Jude? Neither of them had overtly said, one way or the other, though they sat in the Sullivan pew of a Sunday morning.

"So... Montana?" Cadence prodded.

"It's an option," he admitted. "Much as Past Me would laugh uproariously at the thought."

She chuckled. "Me, too. I like it here." Her foot hooked around his in the cool water as her fingers tangled with his. "But then, I've always liked horses."

Graham's shoulder still twinged from his earlier spill. "It wasn't Ranger's fault today."

"He sensed what was going on with that skunk before we did." She angled to look up at him. "Will you ride him again?"

"Ranger? Not for a very, very long time. Another horse, maybe, but not him."

"Tomorrow evening?"

"With you?" He squeezed her hand. "With you by my side, I'll do anything."

Cadence quirked a grin as she tilted her head to one side.

"Almost anything," he amended.

And then he kissed the smirk right off her face.

"I HEARD ABOUT YOUR RIDE TODAY." Paisley bounced out of her seat when Cadence entered the duplex after the moon had risen.

Cadence groaned. "That skunk. Ugh."

"The story was more about you and Graham, but I haven't seen you since to verify."

Cadence's eyebrows angled up. "Weston gossiped to you? He wasn't even there."

"Weston." Paisley nearly spat the cowboy's name. "No,

252

Tyler told me Graham landed in the dirt and you were all googly-eyed at each other. Tell. Me. Everything."

A soft sigh sifted through the air. Had that sound come from Cadence? It must have, because her roommate stared at her with a bemused expression.

"You guys are together. Finally."

"Together." What a beautiful word. "He's amazing. He's everything I always wanted. And he loves me."

"Yay!" Paisley bounced on her toes. "You guys are too cute. What did it? The hashtags?"

"They didn't hurt, but he was finally ready to speak out. And, honestly, so was I. We've been dancing around for weeks, both afraid to face each other at the same time."

Paisley rolled her eyes. "Tell me. It's been so incredibly frustrating to watch. I mean, he was so obviously interested."

"I didn't trust him. And I was afraid."

"And he didn't trust you. And he was afraid."

"Yeah." Cadence sighed.

"I'd like to kick Paul where it hurts."

Wouldn't that be a sight? Cadence couldn't help laughing. "Wearing your pointy cowboy boots, I presume?"

"What else? Not my flip flops, that's for certain."

"Man, I'm so thankful I ended up rooming with you." Even though the chaos in the duplex had never quite subsided, at least her loft was usually orderly.

"Me, too. I should thank Mr. Sullivan sometime."

"It was Tate."

"Well, he's a Mr. Sullivan, too."

"True." Cadence hadn't spent much time with Tate, partly because she'd avoided the office and Graham so much in the past couple of months. Stephanie and Jamie were often in the dining room at mealtime, but they didn't sit at the staff table.

"You heard Stephanie is pregnant?"

"Yeah, I heard. Good for them. And they're breaking ground for a house down the lane. So, that's cool." Would Graham want to do the same thing? A little thrill ran through Cadence at the thought.

Graham Sullivan loved *her*, Cadence Foster.

Would that lead to a proposal? Marriage? A family? A true home in Montana?

"Maybe that will soon be you."

"I'm not counting my chickens before they hatch."

Paisley laughed. "Look at you, turning into a country girl."

"Ha, ha. But it's still a good analogy."

"I want to be your maid of honor."

"You've got it. At least, if I marry Graham." That delightful shiver ran her spine again.

"You thinking of marrying anyone else?"

"Oh, I don't know." Cadence tapped her chin, watching her roommate obliquely. "There are a lot of cute single guys around here. Weston Kline…"

"Sure." Paisley rolled her eyes. "You're attracted to Weston."

"Why not? What's not to like?"

"He's a total grump."

"He'd smile for the right person."

"Well, that someone isn't you. You've got the geeky accountant all tied up in knots, so I'm not sure what you're trying to prove by pretending you're still playing the field."

"You're being awfully territorial."

"Like you should be."

Cadence nudged Paisley with her elbow. "You've been around watching my mess all summer long, but two can play that game?"

Her roommate studied her through narrowed eyes. "What game are we talking about?"

"You're Miss Know-It-All about my feelings for Graham. About how he feels about me. But I've been watching you, too. When are you going to make your own move? Because it's worth it."

"Hashtags don't cure everything."

"Never said they did. I'm not even sure they helped at all, to be honest. But I'm thinking you're trying to deflect. You do that a lot."

"We were talking about you."

"Uh huh. And now we're talking about you. You and a certain grumpy cowboy."

Paisley shook her head. "He's cute, I'll grant you that. But there's nothing going on, nor will there ever be. Can you imagine me with someone like him? Not a chance."

"Work with this analogy."

Paisley widened her eyes.

"You're like sunshine. Truly, you are. And sunshine dispels shadows. It can send rainclouds scuttling. Also, it makes gorgeous rainbows."

"Are you quite done?"

"For now."

"Good. By the way, I gave my notice to Mr. Sullivan today. He invited me back for next season."

Cadence's gut fell. "You're not leaving!"

"Just told you I was."

"Right, but—"

"But nothing. I told you I was thinking about it."

True. But Cadence hadn't actually believed her.

"So, you'll have this whole duplex to yourself, at least until you marry your accountant." Paisley wrinkled her nose. "Don't do that while I'm away, okay? I mean, I could come back for it, but I'd rather be here to help you plan."

"Then stay."

"Girl, I can't. I really, truly, can't."

"Weston."

Paisley sighed. "There's more to it than him, okay?"

Should Cadence press? But the thin lines of her room-mate's lips told her this wasn't the best time. "Okay. But keep talking to me, okay? Or, you know, start."

"It's only eight months until I come back."

"Ugh. That long?"

"Middle of May is when things ramp back up around here. The ranch doesn't actually need a family activities director between now and then, anyway. The boss man didn't try that hard to get me to stay on."

Which reminded Cadence that she needed to talk to Mr. Sullivan herself. What if he didn't need a social media director, either? He probably didn't. What was she thinking, believing she could stay here year 'round?

She'd get right on that tomorrow. Tonight, she only wanted to savor this new thing with Graham. And thank the good Lord above that they'd both come to their senses and given each other another chance... at the same time.

CHAPTER TWENTY-FIVE

Chicago in December. Ugh. Snow blasted sideways beyond the glass that kept the sub-zero wind from the airport departures area.

Beside Graham, Cadence sighed. "Do we need to be here?"

He chuckled. "You know we do. We might be grown adults, but our parents still expect us home for Christmas." His had certainly made it clear they were not traveling to Montana for the season.

"It's going to be weird."

"I know." Graham squeezed her hand. And he wouldn't be able to protect her, not that anyone should need protecting from her own parents. He'd been used to her living a couple of doors down Hummingbird Lane. For the coming week, she'd be dozens of blocks away. And he wouldn't see her in the office, either.

"Don't abandon me." She leaned against his shoulder.

"I never will." Graham turned and wrapped her tight in the circle of his arms. This trust was not something he'd ever get used to. How had a geeky guy like him become lucky enough to win a smart, beautiful woman like Cadence?

He shook his head. Not lucky. Blessed. Both of them had done a ton of growing spiritually since the June night they'd fled Chicago. Semantics didn't change his deep feeling of unworthiness, but somehow that managed to coexist with a newfound peace.

Graham might not be worthy of Cadence's love. He might not be worthy of God's love, either, but it didn't stop either of them from loving him. And it only deepened his own resolve to keep learning how to live a life of love.

Something his parents and hers had yet to acknowledge they needed, despite a nominal adherence to Christianity.

He spotted the black limo idling in the pickup line and reached for his carry-on. "There's Grandfather's chauffeur now."

"I can't believe your grandfather moved back to Chicago. I thought he might be starting something up with Eleanor."

Graham had thought the same. He'd seen the way Grandfather looked at Eleanor and figured a guy who was eighty wouldn't let grass grow beneath his feet. He'd figured wrong, unless Eleanor had shot Grandfather down? Could be.

He grabbed Cadence's hand as they darted out the sliding door, each dragging a rolling case, and into ice pellets streaming sideways. He opened the limo door for Cadence before Kenneth could do so, thrust both cases inside, and jumped in behind her.

"Brr!" He clapped his mittened hands together.

"Welcome home, Graham." Kenneth's eyes met his in the rearview mirror.

"Thank you. I must admit it doesn't feel like home anymore."

The man's eyes softened with a smile. "Perhaps a December visit isn't the best time for a trip down memory lane."

Graham doubted the season made the difference, but there was no need to be argumentative. "Perhaps. First, we're headed to Daniel and Amelia Fosters' home in Hinsdale. Do you have the address?"

"Yes, sir. It's plugged in."

Graham settled into his seat and tugged off the woolen mittens Eleanor had knitted for each of the Sullivan grandsons. For the next ten days, the mitts and his down parka would live in his closet, and he'd get to wear his lined leather gloves and wool trench coat like a proper urban businessman. His jeans, Henleys, and the flannel shirts he'd taken to wearing around the ranch would make way for dress slacks and button-downs.

If he had any friends in the city, they'd never recognize the Montana version of Graham. Moot point. He had no true friends here.

Who knew his cousins would become real friends, though, after all these years? And there were other guys, too. Jordan and some of the others on Maxwell's construction crew had become sociable now that the crush of tourists had lessened over the slow season.

Cadence threaded her fingers through his and leaned on his shoulder.

He closed his eyes for a few seconds. *Thank You, God, for mercies great and small.* "You okay?"

"I think so, but I can hardly wait until next time I see this airport in ten days."

"I know what you mean." Graham chuckled. "But the time will go quickly. We've got tickets for the philharmonic, and we'll walk the Magnificent Mile and Navy Pier. I refuse to let your parents take up all your time, even if it is Christmas in a few days."

"I look forward to it."

Graham's phone chimed with an incoming text. He flicked it on and frowned at the message from his mom.

> We are invited to your cousin Paul's wedding on New Year's Eve, and I expect you to be in attendance.

What on earth? He tilted the device toward Cadence. "Heard anything about this?"

Her eyes grew wide as she read. "You're kidding me, right?"

"I don't think so." He tapped back.

> We landed and are in the limo with Kenneth, dropping Cadence off before I'll be at your place. Please send Aunt Frances my regrets. Cadence and I are booked on flights to Missoula on the 29th.

> Change them.

> Sorry, I can't. You know how packed flights are over the holidays.

Get your uncle to fly you in the private jet.

Mom? I don't want to go to Paul's
wedding, and I'm not going to. Who is he
marrying, anyway?

Dahlia Casselman.

Graham couldn't help the laughter that bubbled up. He
tapped back, *good for him*, before turning off his phone and
pocketing it.

"Dahlia? Seriously? Isn't she the ditzy thing that tried to
glom onto Tate last summer at the Gala of the Stars?"

"The very same."

Cadence bit her lip and looked up at Graham. "Is it
absolutely terrible of me to be happy for them? At least, no
one will expect me to get back with Paul now. Even my
parents will have to give it up for a lost cause."

"I thought they'd stopped harassing you about him."
Graham frowned.

"Kind of? But only because I could stop responding to
texts or abruptly end a phone call if his name came up. I'll
be their captive audience for the next ten days, so I've been
bracing myself."

Graham toyed with her fingers and watched the city
flow by as they drove south. He wouldn't let the circumstances change his timeline, but it sure was a temptation.

No. He had a plan, and he was sticking to it.

ONE OF THE few remnants of Mom's Icelandic upbringing was celebrating Christmas on the 24th with Jolabokaflod, loosely translatable into English as joyous book flood. Cadence had dragged Graham into more bookstores than she could count trying to find the right titles to gift her parents. Dad was always up for the newest political thriller, while Mom pretended not be a reader.

After much deliberation, Cadence picked a devotional for her mother. She'd taken her time decision-making mostly to keep an eye on where Graham seemed to be most interested. Could she complain about the fact that her adorable boyfriend focused on helping her buy gifts for her parents without leaving her side?

But on their long evenings reading in his duplex over the past few months, she'd noted his preferred genres and even series. And now she could sneak off and pick up the newest one for him, hoping against hope he hadn't already snagged it, and she hadn't been observant enough to notice.

He'd be arriving any minute for their family evening. Even though he'd come and gone over the past few days, she'd never see him at the door without remembering him with water dripping off his body that June evening. Thank the Lord Graham had come and saved her from a nasty fate. Also, she should pray for Dahlia, though it seemed like maybe she and Paul were two of a kind and deserved each other.

"You don't need to watch the door." Mom stood across the foyer, arms crossed. "He'll get here when he gets here."

"I know, but I can't wait to see him again." And kiss him.

"You were out with him this morning."

"I love him so much, I can hardly stand it." Cadence studied her mother. Should she go for it? "Like you love Daddy. I know you miss each other when you're apart."

They'd been separated for three months while Mom was in rehab this fall. Cadence could only hope and pray the therapy had been successful, because she'd read the relapse rate was high.

Mom sighed. "Well, I can't stop you from it, I suppose. At least he's rich."

"That's the least of the reasons I love him." Although it didn't hurt. "He's funny. He's kind. He's smart."

"That's nice. I just wish…" Mom pursed her lips.

Not this again. "I think you know that Paul and I were never right for each other. And I know that whole debacle forced you to face your gambling addiction—"

"We don't talk about it."

Cadence straightened her back. "But we should, because hiding problems isn't healthy."

"Now you think you're smarter than your parents."

"I didn't say that." But it did make her worry about how long her mom could hold out. At least they wouldn't lose the house next time her mom bet big. Cadence had thought about signing it over to her dad, but not if they were keeping secrets together. Then neither could be trusted. Her gut twisted.

The chime sounded, and she pivoted back to open the door. Oh, man, her beloved looked good even in his urban duds. They couldn't cover the dark curls or his sparkling blue eyes or his lean physique. "Graham!"

"Happy Jolabokaflod, sweetheart." He kissed her lightly,

caressing her with his gaze, before turning to her mother. "Happy Jolabokaflod, Mrs. Foster."

"Same to you, Graham. Please come in."

Bless Mom. She was trying to accept Cadence's choice. Possibly only because Paul was marrying Dahlia in a few days.

Graham entered the foyer before setting down two enormous shopping bags.

Cadence took his coat as he toed off his boots. Those bags looked mighty large — to say nothing of light — for a few books. And what she wanted for Christmas this year was smaller even than a hardback.

But could she trust Graham? Absolutely. Maybe he'd also brought over Christmas morning gifts tonight. That was probably it.

"You can take your bags into the family room. Mom and I will go grab the trays with hot chocolate and vinertarta and be right in. Dad's there already."

He grinned and nodded as he turned away, bags in tow.

"You did tell him tonight is about books." Mom scowled as they headed to the kitchen.

"I did."

Mom pursed her lips. She didn't need to say more to let Cadence know she wasn't amused that someone would disregard their family tradition. Either Graham would prove himself trustworthy to her parents, or he wouldn't. It didn't change — couldn't change — how she felt about him. He was a winner, no matter what they thought.

Cadence carried the tray of vinertarta, a festive layered cake Mom always picked up at the local Icelandic grocery.

The slices were surrounded by professionally decorated cookies that would taste of preservatives. The cake, however, would taste of a lifetime of Christmas Eves. She hadn't seen an Icelandic bakery in western Montana. Maybe she'd need to learn how to make this delicacy herself.

Back at Sweet River Ranch, Nadine had been baking a glorious array of cookies and treats, everything from gingerbread men to cinnamon shortbread to cranberry pie. Those staying at the resort over the holidays were going to eat well.

Now, Cadence rested the tray on the antique coffee table. Next to it, Mom set down hers, loaded with four mugs of hot chocolate mounded with mini marshmallows. The towering white tree in front of the window was decorated in red balls and bows this year. Orchestral Christmas music flowed gently from the speakers.

Graham looked yummy in a dark green sweater with silver threads and black... jeans? That was a new look for him, but she liked the compromise. Liked that he hadn't forgotten all the ways he'd loosened up since moving to Montana nearly nine months ago. He'd left off his glasses, so he must have picked up new contacts. His eyes were gorgeous, either way, as he smiled at her and patted the seat of the white sofa beside him.

Gratefully, she sank against him and nestled under his arm. If her parents didn't want to see the love she and Graham shared, they didn't have to look.

"Well, here we are." Dad looked at Mom as though helpless to figure out how to proceed with a fourth person in the room.

"Indeed." Mom sat primly on a slipper chair. "Graham, may we ask you to read the Christmas story?"

"Absolutely." If he was surprised, he didn't show it. He simply shifted to pull his phone out of his hip pocket. In no time flat, he was reading the precious story from Luke chapter two.

Cadence listened with her eyes closed, then Graham's words echoed in the still room.

But Mary treasured up all these things, pondering them in her heart.

Cadence had a lot to ponder, too. The birth of the Savior seemed all the more poignant this year as she'd watched Stephanie's abdomen swell with her and Tate's firstborn. They'd spent time together through the fall and become friends.

Graham offered a prayer for blessing without being invited to, as though he figured it was part of the reading. And why not? Then he reached for his bags. "I'm sure you're wondering what oversized books I must have brought tonight, but... allow me?" He passed pillow-shaped packages to Dad, then to Mom, and then to Cadence. "Go ahead."

Mom and Dad looked at each other, shrugged, and began to open them. Cadence did, too, allowing her parents to get ahead of her while she kept a covert eye on progress.

"Oh!" Mom pulled a fuzzy red blanket covered with white snowflakes out of her package. "It's... soft. Thank you."

"You're welcome. I figure books and winter require blankets."

Dad's was navy with the same design as Mom's. Cadence peeked at hers, a pale blue with red-and-white candy canes. She hugged it close. "Thanks, Graham. But you'll be the only one without a blanket to snuggle under later during reading time."

He winked. "Yours might be big enough for two."

Heat flushed her face. "It might."

Cadence sipped her hot chocolate as they began to open books. Her parents oohed and ahed over the ones she'd bought them, and they'd picked up one from her favorite fantasy series for her.

Graham handed packages to each of her parents, this time in appropriate shapes. He hadn't asked her their reading taste, come to think of it. But he may have perused the display cases in the living room on one of his visits this week. What had he picked?

Dad pulled out a copy of "In-Laws Are Better Than Outlaws" as Mom opened "Prayers for Your Newlywed Daughter." They both gaped at Graham. Then at her.

And then Graham was on one knee in front of her, clutching a small gold book in his hands. "Merry Christmas, Cadence. This one is for you."

With quaking hands, she took it from his hands and read the title: "Will You Marry Me?" It was too light to be even a paperback. She opened the book-shaped gift box to see a velvet nest inside. Her gaze flew to meet Graham's.

"Will you? Will you marry me?" His voice all but broke on his question. His eyes pleaded with hers.

"Oh, Graham. Yes!"

He tugged out the princess-cut diamond with its platinum band. It was the most beautiful thing she'd ever seen.

Smaller than Paul's ring she'd worn for over a year, but ever so much more exquisite. "It's beautiful."

"You're far more beautiful." His trembling fingers managed to transfer the ring from the box to her finger. Then he kissed her knuckles before looking back at her. "I love you so much, Cadence. I can't begin to tell you. But I've got the rest of our lives to show you, every single day, exactly what you mean to me."

Then he gathered her into his arms and kissed her.

"I love you, Graham. Thank you, thank you, thank you."

A whisper of sound caught her attention, and she glanced up to see her parents tiptoeing out of the room, arm in arm.

EPILOGUE

I f Weston hadn't been dying of curiosity — and if his mother hadn't made him — he'd have skipped the party at Tate and Stephanie's new house. They'd moved in mere days before their baby boy, Simon Peter Sullivan, had made his entrance.

Weston wasn't into babies, though Jamie was cute enough, he supposed. But everyone else was gaga over the whimpering infant. Especially Mom.

She turned to him with the baby cradled in her arms. "Want to hold him?"

He backed up. "No, thanks. That's okay. Let someone else." *Someone who wants to.* But he didn't dare tell her that.

"He's so precious." Mom smooched Simon's face about a dozen times. Poor kid yawned and squirmed as though bored of the whole thing.

Had Mom kissed him or Jude like that when they were newborns? Jude, maybe. Weston's little brother had always been the more adorable of the two.

"Is it my turn yet?" Cadence sidled up beside Mom, who

turned and placed Simon in her arms. "Oh, look, Graham. Can you imagine anything so tiny, so perfect?"

Seriously? Weston managed not to roll his eyes... outwardly, at least. Why did people talk like that? She was holding the baby. He was tiny. No imagination needed.

She and Graham were planning a September wedding here at the ranch. Was there any way Weston could be somewhere else right then? Because weddings were as bad as babies. Possibly worse. Neither was something that would ever happen to him.

Jude came up beside him and poked him with an elbow. "Hey."

His brother spoke his language. "Hey to you, too."

"Nice house, huh?" Jude looked appreciatively around the great room with its tall ceiling and stone fireplace.

"Sure." Twice as nice as the ranch house where they'd grown up. Five times as nice as anything he'd lived in since. But according to the Sullivans, it was quite a comedown from what they were used to. Tate's father — Weston couldn't think of the man as his own uncle — kept saying things like, "are you sure it's big enough?" and, "it's not bad for a cottage."

It might be a full year now since Weston had met his maternal grandfather and agreed to work for him and see how the other half lived. The rich half.

Whoever would have guessed that the family Weston had never known was practically made of gold coins? It was intriguing. Attractive. And also, off-putting.

Because he knew he'd never truly fit in. He didn't have the education, the social skills, the... everything the Sullivan cousins had been raised with.

"Soon the ranch will be buzzing again." Jude rocked back on his heels and grinned.

Paisley Teele would be back in mere weeks. Hers was the only name Weston had been watching for in recent staff meetings.

He wasn't sure how he felt about her return. She had been so determined to get through his shell that he'd had to constantly rebuild the barricade to keep her out. What had made her decide to take him on as a project?

He resented it.

But she intrigued him, too. What if he let himself actually feel?

Nope. Far too risky. What if she found out the things he'd kept hidden from everyone, including Mom and Jude? She'd run, for sure.

Might be worth telling her, in that case.

Because Weston Kline might not be better off without her, but Paisley Teele was definitely better off without him.

She just didn't know it yet.

A NOTE...

Dear Weston,

I'm looking forward to digging beneath that prickly surface and finding out what makes you tick... and yes, I can hear you groan from here. You might not think you want to be loved, but you do, and you want Paisley to be the one to do the loving.

You two are going to present quite the challenge, but I have ideas. And no, you may not ride off on Ranger and avoid the whole experience. See you soon!

Your loving author, Valerie

Dear Reader,

I hope you loved Cadence and Graham and understood how their wishy-washiness came from deeply rooted insecurity. I love-love-loved getting to know this jilted bride and her rescuer, and I hope you did, too.

Why not read Weston and Paisley's story, *A Sunny Sweetheart for the Cowboy*, next?

I look forward to meeting you again soon in the log lodge at Sweet River Ranch.

Blessings, Valerie

Psst: Reviews are awesome, too...

ACKNOWLEDGMENTS

Thank you, dear reader, for loving all of the Montana Ranches Christian Romance series: Saddle Springs, Cavanagh Cowboys, and now Sweet River! I'm excited to write the stories of the other four Sullivan grandsons in the next year or so.

Thanks to my author buddies Elizabeth Maddrey, Lynnette Bonner, and Jan Thompson for writing sprints and accountability. Friends make such a difference.

My amazing editor, Nicole, has been with me from the beginning. I am so thankful for her!

I'm also grateful for the Christian Indie Authors Facebook group and my sister bloggers at Inspy Romance. These folks make a difference in my life every single day. I'm thrilled to walk beside them as we tell stories for Jesus!

Thank you to my Facebook friends, followers, street team, and reader group members for prayers, encouragement, and great fellowship. If you'd like to join other readers who love my stories, please find us at Valerie Comer: Readers Group. This crew helped me title the books Graham gave Cadence's parents on Christmas Eve, and we have loads of other fun as well.

Thanks to my husband, Jim, whose love for me never fails and who encourages me in every endeavor. Thanks to my kids, their spouses, and my wonderful grandkids for cheering me on. To them, having an author for a mom/grandma is "normal." Imagine that!

All my love and gratitude goes to Jesus, the One who is my vision, the High King of Heaven, the lord of my heart. Thank You. A thousand times, thank You.

BOOKS BY VALERIE COMER

You'll find the complete list of titles by Valerie Comer on her website: fifty books (and counting) in ten series! Come on over to find farm-fresh romance, cowboy romance, and small-town romance, all with distinctly Christian themes.

https://valeriecomer.com/books

ABOUT VALERIE COMER

Valerie Comer is constantly amazed that living, talking, dreaming characters appear in her mind and flow from her fingertips and, from there, to her delighted readers. She only hopes her creations enjoy their happily-ever-afters as much as she does hers, sharing rural life in western Canada with her husband, adult children, and adorable grandkids.

Valerie is a two-time *USA Today* bestselling author and a two-time Word Award winner. She is known for writing engaging characters, strong communities, and deep faith into her green clean romances.

To find out more, visit her website at www.valeriecomer.com, where you can read her blog, explore her many links, and sign up for her email newsletter, where you will find news, giveaways, deals, book recommendations and more. You can also find Valerie blogging with other authors of Christian contemporary romance at Inspy Romance.